I0557624

# THE OTHER HALF OF ME

*The Coming Home Series*

## JENNIFER SIVEC

Edited by
**JC WING**

Illustrated by
**JM WALKER**

*"In all the world, there is no heart for me like yours. In all the world, there is no love for you like mine."*
— *Maya Angelou*

# THE DREAM

M aggie

I'VE ALWAYS HAD THE SAME DREAM, FOR AS LONG AS I CAN remember, but no matter what I do, I can't make it come to me when I want to. It appears when it wants, teasing and hinting at something that I don't understand.

It's always exactly the same.

I'm standing on the edge of a place I don't understand, while a soft white cloud seems to dance around them, leaving them floating in front of me. The only thing I see is them, hovering close but not to close to one another, seemingly afraid to be too far apart. I realize they are young; far too young for the heaviness of the emotion that sweeps in and out of the cloud, but it seems true and real, and I am drawn to them by an intensity that I don't recognize.

A boy, about the age of six, with eyes as deep and blue as I have ever seen, and a little girl of the same age, with light brown ringlets and a smile that can light up the darkest corner of the earth, approach one another. She is cautious, but he runs up to her, stopping only a foot away.

"I'm here now," he says, proud and breathless as though he has travelled far to get here.

"I don't care." Her eyes are dark and emotionless, and for a moment I am frozen with fear.

He pauses and I wait for him to answer, anticipating pain in his response. Instead he smiles, his lips parted wide, his two top teeth missing, giving him an impish grin.

"Yes, you do." He places a kiss lightly on her cheek, but she pulls away.

"No," she protests.

"You forget every time," he says, laughing.

"Forget what?" she asks, intrigued by the sound of his laughter.

"Me." He runs his fingers down her cheek, and she doesn't pull away.

"I don't forget you." Her voice is soft, but there is pain, and as hard as I try to look away, I cannot. I feel like an intruder on their moment, but the tugging of my heart tells me that I belong here, too. The girl is familiar to me, and I know her as well as I know myself. I feel her fear and anger, and the butterflies fluttering in her stomach are also in mine.

"Then what is it?" he asks, his voice not belonging to a six-year-boy.

"I'm angry ... with you for leaving me," she says, her bottom lip quivering. "Why didn't you stay?"

"You know why ..."

"I don't care. I don't want you to leave. It always hurts, and I need you."

"I have to go, and so do you, but we always make it back to each other."

"I don't care. I don't want to do it anymore. It makes me

too sad." She turns her back on him, swiping at the tears that are falling down her soft cheeks. "I just want to stay with you."

"This is how it's always been. You know this, but I love you," he says to her as though they are in mid-conversation and he is persuading her. He holds her hand gently, caressing it softly with his own.

"I don't know you," she says suddenly, taking a step back and pulling her hand away from him.

"Yes, you do," he kneels down next to her on one knee. "You know me. You've always known me."

"No, I don't know you. Not anymore," she says, her dark eyes resolute as her lips are fixed in a stubborn line on her pretty face.

"Nothing has changed between us. I'm the same person I've always been, and so are you." He touches her chin with his thumb, and against her will, her eyes find his.

"How did you find me?" she asks, turning toward him fully, allowing him to hold both of her hands in his.

"I'll always find you, or you'll find me no matter where we are," he says, simply, innocence bursting from his shining eyes, a smile playing on his lips.

"Aren't you always looking for me?" He moves so close to her that they are nearly nose-to-nose.

"Yes, but how ..." she says, confusion nearly taking her over.

"Because of who you are."

"Who I am?" She tries to take a step away from him, but he holds her with his eyes.

"You know. Don't you feel it in here?" he asks, pointing to his heart.

"Yes." She hesitates, speaking slowing. "Who am I?"

"You know."

"No, I don't know."

Suddenly, I realize that I'm no longer an observer. Her voice is coming from my mouth, and her heart is pounding so hard in my chest. I can see him through her eyes, and I understand that I'm her, and he is looking directly at me.

"Yes ... listen to what's inside of you. What has always been inside of you."

As quickly as he says it, I know who I am, and instantly I know how he finds me, as though he has an internal compass that has a direct connection to my heart.

"Yes ..." he says, his voice urging me on.

"I'm you," I whisper.

"Yes."

"... and you're me."

"Yes."

"You're my other half."

"Yes."

I AWAKEN FROM THE DREAM, MY HEART SPLIT IN TWO, ALL my pain and anguish spilling out. His absence is so real, and the emptiness resounds throughout my soul.

The dream never changes, and the story never shifts. I remain broken because he isn't with me, and I wonder if I'll ever find the beautiful blue-eyed man who claims to be the other half of me.

## 2

# RECOGNITION

S am

I RECOGNIZED HER THE MOMENT I SAW HER.

I had never seen her before, but something about her called out to me, and the pull was so strong. Magnetic. It was the beginning of the semester, and she was in my Trig Two class. She walked in, and something inside of me instantly stopped.

It was as though all the air was sucked out of the room, and even though it was sappy as hell, I couldn't deny it. I waited for her to see me, but she didn't. Once she looked up, she didn't even look around, her dark eyes fixed on the front of the class, her hands constantly fiddling with her soft curls. I couldn't stop thinking about burying my hands in those curls as I looked at her out of the corner of my eye from two chairs over.

I could tell by the way she kept her head down and didn't

talk to anyone that she was shy, maybe even damaged, and I was hooked. I loved damaged. I craved it. I needed to know more about her. She wasn't your typical loner. She was beautiful, and when she walked through a crowd, she didn't even realize that there was a group of guys staring at her ass and waiting for her to notice them.

There was something about her that kept people away, and she existed with an invisible perimeter surrounding her that kept everyone else out. I watched her to see if she spoke to anyone, but everything was on a need basis only. She only spoke to those she had to, but always kept a perimeter around her. Otherwise, she was on her own, existing in her own bubble, completely isolated from anyone else around her. She didn't even have regular friends, like most of the girls our age.

From what I could tell, she had no one.

It was intriguing and intimidating, but I was drawn to her for reasons I couldn't explain. Something inside told me that she would let me in. "Just try," the voice in my head told me. "Just talk to her, and she'll talk back."

I'd never felt anything like it before. I wasn't the guy who fell all over girls. I was the opposite. They made fools out of themselves trying to get into my bed, and it was always easy, mostly fun, but empty. It had been the same since high school, and college had been even easier. My mom told me it was because girls always liked the bad boys, the ones who were unattainable. It had been the same for her.

I wasn't complaining. I loved that it was so easy. Soft skin, warm lips, hips eager to push against mine, jeans easily unbuttoned, but it was always the same. I never felt anything but the most basic desire, and I never felt anything after. I couldn't wait for them to leave, even though they did their best to stay. In the end, they ended up hurrying out, sometimes not even completely dressed, and often swearing my name.

Yet, they always came back anytime I wanted them to. That was until I saw Maggie, and I knew instantly that she was different. Something about the huskiness of her voice drew my attention to her and sent little electrical charges through me. She wasn't like most of them with her conservative soft tee shirts and casual long dark skirts that didn't draw attention to her at all. She was obscure and did her best to disappear, and if I wasn't so damned attracted to her, I wouldn't have even known that she existed.

I'd spent most of my life alone, too, and I recognized the loneliness in her. I could tell that we were the same, and even though her past might have been much cleaner than mine, I instantly knew who she was and what she'd been though.

Its more than just the challenge, I told myself. There had been plenty of girls in the past who'd bested me. This was more than just an acquisition.

She was something else entirely.

I watched her for the entire semester, practically failing out of the class because I was so preoccupied. I couldn't explain it, but I had to know her, and I had to talk to her. I had to be near her, and over time, I found myself slipping nearer to her every chance I got, following her around like a damned ghost.

## 3

# THE LONG TRIP

M aggie

FOR AS LONG AS I COULD REMEMBER, I ALWAYS FELT AS
though part of me was missing, like I was missing a limb, or
an organ. I could never explain it to anyone, and I never even
tried, keeping it to myself as I did everything else.

I had tried to tell my mother how I felt once when I was
eight, but she didn't believe in things like that. She only
believed in what could be seen. Feelings were wasted on her,
and she explained it away as a sign of weakness, adding it to
the long list of those that she saw in me.

"You can't possibly be missing anything, Margaret. You're
entirely too young to have any idea what you're talking
about."

"Mom ... " I protested. "Something is wrong with me ... I
feel it ... inside."

"You're being silly. You're too young to have any idea what

you're talking about." She pushed her hair back behind her ear like she did when she was annoyed.

I'm sure I tried to argue with her, but it never mattered. Arguing with her was pointless. She never cared what I said. It wouldn't matter to her that the emptiness inside felt like a pit deep in my stomach. It was a never-ending abyss that I couldn't express, and I knew that if my own mother wouldn't care to understand it, nobody would.

When I was fourteen, my entire life became an exercise in avoiding anything that would make me look or feel any more awkward than I already was. I was a gangly, braces-wearing, clumsy girl who was struggling through high school. I huddled in my own little corner of the world and hid in the library every chance I could with the librarian, Miss Ryan, who recognized a little bit of herself in me and often told me so.

I was an utter disappointment to my mother, and it resonated from her beautiful brown eyes every time she looked at me. She was a natural beauty with blonde hair, who made being beautiful look easy, and when I looked in the mirror at my flat chest and acne-covered face, I knew that I didn't resemble her in any way. I couldn't imagine _her_ ever feeling the way I did, wishing that I could just be absorbed into the wall of books and disappear.

Life was lonely until I was fifteen and met Trip. Tall, quiet, and handsome Trip. He didn't fit in either, shunning every group that tried to include him. He seemed to have contempt for anyone who tried to talk to him, but for reasons I couldn't understand, he took an interest in me, and I found myself in unfamiliar territory, an onslaught of emotions overcoming me, making it difficult to breathe.

"I just want to be your friend," he'd said, and I believed him. His green eyes were earnest and pulled me in, making me feel uncomfortable. Even though the acne was clearing up, and my breasts were finally starting to develop, I was quiet and shy. He was the first boy to pay attention to me, and I ignored the little voice that tugged at me and told me to stay away.

I did everything I could for a long time to erase Trip's memory from my mind but, nothing worked ... until Sam.

## ❧  4  ❧

# BROKEN

# M aggie

I ALWAYS THOUGHT THAT I WAS A SMART GIRL, DESPITE
what my mother had been telling me my entire life.

That was, until I met Trip.

Admittedly awkward and self-conscious, I was finally
fifteen, almost able to drive and growing out of my ugly-duck-
ling phase. My hair was soft and no longer greasy, the acne
drying up, and for the first time I was filling out my bras. Trip
was the first boy that I was ever friends with. He was tall,
rebellious, and for some strange reason he talked to me when
the rest of the boys completely ignored me. I'd decided that I
liked him, even though I didn't really know him.

"You get me, Maggie," he said the first time we spoke. He
was alone at lunch and so was I, and he sat at my table, immediately going on a strange rant about politics and govern-
ment. It didn't seem to matter to him that I was the only one

who was listening. He just spoke as I sat in silence, eating my turkey sandwich, chewing slowly as I tried to understand what he was saying. I had learned early in life not to talk too much, so I became a far better listener than a talker, and Trip liked that about me.

I'd nodded, admiring his sandy hair and green eyes. He was cute in a strange way, and I often caught him looking at me, which made my insides flutter.

We began to spend a lot of time together.

"He's a weird boy, Margaret," my mother said one night after he left our house after we'd studied together. "He's not a normal boy his age, and I don't know if I like you spending so much time with him."

"He's nice, and he's my friend," I'd said defensively. She never approved of much where I was concerned, and I was irritated but not surprised that she didn't like Trip.

"I ... just don't trust him. He's not ... normal."

The more she disliked him, the more intriguing I found him to be. He was the only one who really talked to me, and when I spoke, he listened.

More importantly, he wanted to kiss me. I knew by how he stared at my lips and would lick his own. I wasn't sure that I wanted to kiss him, but to have someone who wanted to kiss me was enticing.

"Have you ever kissed anyone, Maggie?" he'd asked, one afternoon when we'd been studying in his room. Usually, we studied at my house because his was too loud, but his family was gone, so we decided to study at his instead.

I shook my head.

He smiled at me, a glint in his eyes that I didn't recognize. I'd thought about kissing but had never done it. When I saw kissing in the movies, or read about it in a book, my heart skipped and something deep in my private areas seemed to wake up. I'd wanted to kiss someone, but had never met anyone I wanted to. I wasn't even sure if I wanted to kiss him, but I liked him enough to try.

"Do you want to kiss me?" he asked, moving closer to me, putting his hand gently on my knee. His face was inches from mine, and I could feel his breath on my cheek.

I nodded, closing my eyes.

"Do you want to touch me?" he asked, his eyes large as he grabbed my hand and guided it toward his crotch.

I pulled my hand back. No, I shook my head as I felt him chuckle in my ear.

His hand began to wander over my back and sides as I shifted uncomfortably. His touch was gentle as he explored, his breath coming quicker. I had never had a boy touch me before as I sat stone still, waiting to see where his hands would go, ready to push him away at any moment.

He groaned as I opened my eyes and watched as he began to rub himself. I closed my eyes and squeezed them tight, and before I knew it, his lips were on mine, and he was shoving his tongue in my mouth. It was wet and slightly slimy as it darted in and out of my lips, rapidly over and over.

"Maggie, I want you so much," he breathed.

In a flurry of activity, I felt his hand moving up my thighs until one of his hands was on my back while the other was suddenly between my legs, rubbing awkwardly.

"Please, stop," I said, trying to grab his hand. He forced his fingers in harder as I felt a sharp pain.

"No!" I grabbed his wrist, trying to pull his arm back. He fumbled at the snap on the top of my jeans and tried to shove his hand in the waistband.

"Stop, Trip!" I fought against his mouth, trying to push his hand away. He was stronger than I'd ever realized, and I felt myself begin to panic as his hand made its way further down, his fingers touching my soft sensitive flesh.

"I said stop, dammit!" I stood up and pushed him away,

forcefully, managing to push him over. He fell on the floor and jumped up immediately, his face red as he panted.

"I have to go," I said, my face flushing as I grabbed my books and started for the door.

"Maggie, stop, I'm sorry! I got carried away."

I turned around briefly and saw that he was aroused, then continued to run as fast as I could.

I realized as I ran that I'd never wanted to kiss him in the first place and never wanted to again.

*

I STAYED AWAY FROM HIM FOR WEEKS, REFUSING HIS CALLS.

The feel of his hands touching me stayed with me, and I shuddered when I thought of it. I felt violated, never imaging that anyone would be so forceful with me. My mother had been right; there was something strange about him, and the frantic look in his eyes when he touched me was burned in my brain.

"I'm sorry" he texted repeatedly. "It'll never happen again. I got carried away. Please forgive me."

He had been my only real friend, and as I went about my days mostly alone, I realized that I missed him. After all, I'd agreed to kiss him, not knowing that it would go so far. I realized that it had been my fault for leading him on and decided that I wouldn't put him in that position again. I ignored the voice that nagged at me to stay away and convinced myself that we could just be friends.

I texted him after a month, and he was ecstatic.

"I'm sorry, Maggie. You know I would never hurt you," he said earnestly. "You're just so beautiful, I couldn't help myself, but it'll never happen again, I swear." His green eyes were clear, and we sealed our friendship with a laugh and a handshake.

We began to spend time together again, mostly studying, going to the movies on occasion, and just hanging out. After a few months, the awkwardness of the incident behind us, I forgot that it had ever happened, and we became more comfortable with one another.

The last night of our freshman year, he invited me over to celebrate with our favorite horror movie and popcorn.

When I walked into his house it was empty.

"Where is everyone?" I asked, unaccustomed to the quiet. With two brothers and a sister, there was usually a flurry of activity in his house.

"Remember when I told you that I had a surprise? The surprise is, they're all camping for the weekend! We have the house to ourselves." He smiled, ushering me in and closing the door behind me. "We can finally watch a movie in peace without being interrupted twenty times."

My heart rate sped up. It's okay, I told myself, immediately feeling silly. He hadn't so much as even tried to hold my hand since we had reconciled, and I chastised myself for being such a baby.

"Cool," I said, hoping that I sounded happier than I felt.

As we settled onto the couch for the movie, I made sure to keep space between us on the couch. As the movie began, I could see his profile in the dark, and began to breathe easier.

"You know that I'm really a good guy, don't you?" Trip said, staring straight ahead.

"Yes," I said, my voice low.

"I would never hurt you." I felt his fingers on my neck, rubbing gently. His other hand grabbed mine.

"I know," I said, my skin tingling with fear.

"The last time you acted like I was going to hurt you, or even worse, rape you," he said, edging closer to me.

"Trip, can we just watch the movie?" I asked, trying to keep the desperation from creeping into my voice.

"Sure, Maggie. We can watch the movie ... after ... " he said.

"After what?" I asked, afraid.

Suddenly, his hand was down from my neck and over my breasts. His other hand was squeezing mine hard.

"You promised ..." I said, my chest tight.

"I did, but I've seen how you look at me. You can't deny it. You wouldn't be here if you didn't want me as much as I want you." His fingers had made their way inside my bra and were on my bare skin as I tried to grab his hands.

"Please ... Trip. I didn't come here for this," I begged, trying to squirm away. I realized that I was suddenly feeling very hot and faint.

"Don't fight it, Maggie. You're going to be my first. I always knew you would be." His lips were on my neck as I tried to pull away. He was licking me with his tongue, and it felt like a worm on my skin. The harder I struggled, the more excited he got, and I could tell that he was hard as he pushed against me with his hips. I felt dizzy and realized with horror that I was beginning to fade out. I was losing consciousness, struggling to fight as he pushed me on the couch face-down, shoving my face in the cushions. He began pulling off my pants. My body felt heavy and helpless, but he didn't seem to mind as he maneuvered me with ease. He flipped me over, pulled off my panties and parted my legs, a wild look in his eyes. I could feel his weight on top of me, his mouth on my breasts, and I knew that fighting was useless. I no longer controlled my body as I tried desperately to fight him and stay awake.

I began to fade away, thankful that I could no longer feel the pain of his body violating me as part of me broke apart inside.

Just as everything went black, the only thing I could see was his face twisted above mine, and I knew that nothing would ever be the same again.

❧

I WAS BROKEN.

Trip had broken me.

When I awoke, I was half-clothed, my body sore in all the wrong places, and my head was pounding. I was sluggish and slow, and I realized that he must have drugged me. I stumbled around, searching for the rest of my clothes and purse and found everything but my underwear. I struggled into my jeans and shoes, keeping a frantic eye out for Trip.

Rape.

He had raped me. He had been my friend and had violated me in a way that I hadn't imagined. I should've known what he would do, but I didn't listen to the voice in my head that told me to stay away.

I heard a rustling, and before I could react, Trip's voice was in my ear.

"I had fun. Did you?"

"What did you do to me?" I asked, my voice low.

"I just gave you something to make you ... relax ..." he said, his voice making my skin crawl as he tried to lick my ear. "You needed it."

"You ... What did you do to me? " I sobbed without meaning to.

"I didn't do anything you didn't want me to," he said, smiling. "You've been begging for it since I met you. I could see you always looking at my dick, wanting it. Since nobody else was ever going to touch you, I decided to do you a favor."

"I swear, I didn't want you to do this." I said, angrily.

"You did," he said, leaning in so close that I felt my skin crawl. "You've wanted it since the moment I met you."

"No, I ... just ... we were friends," I tried to sound stronger than I felt.

" You threw yourself at me, flaunting your body at me. What was I supposed to do?" He grabbed the back of my hair and pulled hard, making me yelp. "I only made love to you because I felt sorry for you. If you tell anyone, I'll just tell them what a dirty little whore you are and how you begged me to fuck you. I'll tell them that you begged me for it, and they'll believe me."

I felt as though a knife had been plunged in my heart as I stared at him in disbelief. Deep down, I knew he was right. I had known what he was all about, and somehow, deep inside, I knew what would happen if I was with him when there was nobody around. I was weak and ugly and pathetic, and in the end, I had gotten what I deserved.

I knew that I could never tell anyone what happened because I only had myself to blame.

## 5

### STAY

S am

"Where have you been?" The girl had been looking for me even though I didn't know that I had been lost. "I need you."

"I don't know," I said, keeping my distance from her. She was older than she used to be in my previous dreams, but I knew her immediately. "Why do you always leave me?"

"It's supposed to be this way. I don't know why," she said, trying to get closer to me.

"Why do I always dream about you?"

"The same reason I always dream about you," she said, her pretty brow furrowed.

"It doesn't make any sense. When I'm with you, things seem normal and right. Don't you know that without you I'm alone?" I asked, frustrated.

"Yes, but so am I." Her voice was soothing but ragged. "I'm alone without you."

"Then why aren't we together?" I asked, turning to look at her, her brown eyes melting away my anger. "Why do I only see you in my dreams. Will I ever find you?"

"It'll happen when we're meant to find one another," she said, reaching for me.

"I'm alone without you." I said, something inside aching. "I'm nothing without you."

"Don't say that. You're everything. You'll see."

"I don't even know who in the hell I am without you." I was pleading with her, though I wasn't sure why. She didn't control this.

"We'll find our way." She held me, and I lost myself in her arms. It felt like a promise, and I wanted to beg her to keep it.

"Can't you just stay with me?" I asked.

"Not yet. It's not time, but one day it will be," she said, her soft skin imprisoning me.

"Please ... just stay," I knew I was begging, but I didn't care. "I need you. You don't know what I've been through."

"One day I will," she said, touching my cheek the way she always did, in that lingering way. "One day, I'll stay with you forever, no matter what, but it's not time yet."

I awoke, my pillow wet with tears as I reached across my empty sheets repeating one word over and over.

Stay.

## ❧ *6* ❧
# RUINED

# M aggie

Trip had ruined me for anyone.

I was convinced that I would never love or trust anyone again, and I had managed to remain alone all throughout high school and the first year of college. I didn't trust anyone. I had ignored the voice in my head that warned me to stay away from Trip, and I no longer even trusted myself.

Even though I never spoke to him again after that night, I never told anyone what happened. I had nobody to tell. I was completely and utterly alone, refusing to allow anyone in.

My mother was happy I no longer spent time with Trip, though she didn't understand how I couldn't have anyone else in my life.

"Where are your friends, Margaret? Are you that incapable of making friends that you have nobody? How is that possible? What is wrong with you?"

I had always kept to myself but after Trip, I spent more time in the library alone than I ever had.

"I want to make friends but ... I just can't." I didn't want to tell her that I was more comfortable alone and that I wasn't like the other girls. I didn't want to tell her that talking to others made me anxious and tongue-tied. My mother would never understand. She had never felt that way and talked with everyone. Even when I was in a room full of people I still felt completely alone.

I knew there was something wrong with me, but keeping to myself had always been easier. While other girls were having sleepovers and talking about boys, I was hiding and reading to myself. I didn't want to make friends. I was far happier alone, but after what Trip did to me, I no longer had a choice. Nobody would ever understand how he'd hurt me.

"I blame myself. I should've done better with you." She always shook her head and said it with such regret and remorse. "You're such a pretty girl, but you never smile, and the frown lines are becoming permanently indented in your face. It's aging you, really."

If I was a mess before, I was broken now. Completely and utterly destroyed. His hands on my body had soiled my skin forever and for anyone else who may want to touch me.

I was ruined, and there was nothing anyone could do or would ever do about it.

## 7

# MAGGIE WHITAKER

M aggie

"Hey, you're Maggie Whitaker?" A male voice caught me off guard as I approached my car after my last class on a Wednesday. He was panting slightly as he ran to me, but tried to hide it. I was amused as I realized from the redness on his cheeks and his labored breathing that he must have been chasing me. I wondered for how long and how I hadn't managed to see him. I knew my mother would be so disappointed at my lack of awareness for my surroundings. She would take it as a personal let-down that I hadn't been more aware.

I recognized him immediately, but I knew him only by reputation.

He was the guy every girl on campus wanted to sleep with and every guy wanted to be friends with. He was fun and popular and better looking than most. He drank and partied too much, but he was charming and fun, and there wasn't anyone who ever said anything bad about him, even though it was often agreed that he had a dark side. The females were drawn to it because it made him emotionally inaccessible, and they saw it as a challenge, but the males just ignored it because it made them uncomfortable. Nobody ever went into detail, they just whispered about it when they didn't think anyone was listening.

It was easy to hear things when I was invisible and nobody ever thought I was listening, but I had heard plenty. Enough to be interested just like everyone else, but also enough to know that he would never be interested in someone like me.

I tried to keep my eyes lowered as I stared at him, careful not to appear as nervous as I felt. I averted my eyes from his strong arms that didn't appear cold in the least on such a cool fall day. While everyone else wore jackets and sweaters, he had on a simple gray tee that hugged him in all the right places.

"Yeah, I'm Maggie," I said, startled, but not afraid. I knew he was in a couple of my classes, but we'd never spoken before.

"I hope you don't mind, but I had to chase you down because, well ... you walk fast, and I meant to grab you after class, but all of a sudden you were just gone." The sound of his voice was warm in my ears, and my insides were turning to liquid by the sound of it. I was beginning to see what the talk was all about as he stared down at me.

I tried to avoid his gaze but thought that it couldn't hurt to sneak a peek at him just for a brief moment. I realized quickly that I couldn't have been more wrong as I found myself staring into the most incredible set of blue eyes I had ever seen. They weren't baby blue, or sky blue, they were more like the color of the sea. They were deep, endless and crinkled up beautifully when he smiled, like he was doing right then. I smiled back at him instinctively, which was something I was never inspired to do, but I couldn't help myself. What was wrong with me?

I was cautious with everyone. Yet, there was something about him that didn't frighten me like everyone else did. His eyes were soft and kind unlike the hardness of Trip's green eyes, and I felt myself drawn to him.

"Hey," he said, suddenly looking a little awkward and completely delicious in his worn out jeans that hung just right on his hips and his baseball hat sitting backward on his head. "I'm Sam."

"Hi ... Sam," I said, lowering my eyes so that I wouldn't have to take him in completely. His smile was blinding, and I was afraid to look fully for fear that I might turn into a blubbering idiot.

"Hey," he repeated, without saying another word. He had finally caught his breath and was staring at me, never breaking eye contact. The air between us was thick and palpable, and neither one of us seemed to be willing to break the spell. There was something about him that made me want to say things I had never felt comfortable saying to anyone else in my entire life. He was doing something to me that I had always wanted to be done, always imagined someone doing to me, but had given up hope on.

"Hi." I waited for him to speak, fighting the urge to jump in my car and drive away as fast as I could.

He startled as he realized he had been staring. "I, uh, was ..." He took off his hat and shoved it into his back pocket as he ran his hands through his thick brown hair a few times. He continued to stammer. "Y-Y-You're in my math class, and I'm complete shit at math. In fact, I'm failing it right now along with a couple of other classes ... which I know you don't really care about. But anyway, I've seen you in class, and you seem really smart, and you always have the right answers. I was hoping ... I mean ... can you ... do you think you can help me, because I need to pass this class or I'm screwed."

I paused.

I was smart. As it turned out I was good in math and the other two classes he was failing as well, but I didn't want to seem like I was rubbing it in so I just smiled and nodded. I knew the moment he opened his mouth that there was no other answer than the one I gave him.

"I don't know ..." I remembered the last time I had offered to study with someone, and I hesitated. I didn't know Sam and wondered what he wanted from me.

"I understand, I mean, you don't know me. I get it. You probably think I'm just some asshole trying to sleep with you like everyone else, but I really do need the help. If I don't pass, I'm out. I'll lose my scholarship money, and I won't be able to afford to go to school. I really need the help." Sam spoke rapidly, and I could hear the desperation in his voice.

"Nobody's trying to sleep with me," I said, instantly regretting it.

"How is that possible?" he asked, an adorable sideways grin nearly taking my breath away.

I looked at him, weighing my options. I wanted to help him, but I hadn't been able to help anyone, even myself for as long as I could remember.

"Yes." The word came out of my mouth before I could I stop them.

"Yes? You mean ... you'll help me?" he looked relieved and terrified at the same time.

"Yes," I said not believing it myself. "I'll help you."

"Okay ... I ... I can't pay you ... I mean, for the tutoring," he stammered, his eyes wide.

"You don't have to pay me," I said, clearing my throat and feeling bare, as though he might be able to see my fear. "I have to study anyway."

"Thank you! Damn, I mean, wow. Thank you. I'm so relieved that you'll help me!" he said, letting out a long breath as though he had been holding it the entire time, waiting for me to answer.

We agreed to meet the following day in the library on campus at noon. I tried to convince myself that everything was going to be okay as I fought the urge to hyperventilate. I was terrified as memories of spending time with Trip flooded over me. I was frozen, knowing that I would never be the same.

## ❧ 8 ❧

# AT FIRST SIGHT

S am

I COULD TELL FROM THE MOMENT SHE TURNED AROUND, her brown curls bobbing in the sunlight, that she liked me. I found myself doing everything I could do to make her smile, which wasn't easy.

She gave me a small smile but cautious, reminding me of the sweet abused pup Mom and I had rescued when I was a kid. We named her Macy, and even though she finally trusted us, it took a long time. Damn that dog was skittish, but when I finally won her over, she was 100% mine. That dog was the best thing that ever happened to me when I was younger until she hit by a car, sending me into a tailspin I couldn't recover from for a long time.

Maggie reminded me of Macy.

Skittish but beautiful.

When I asked her to go to the library to help me study, I

thought for sure she'd jump right into her car and pull away as fast as she could, but she paused. Something about that moment when she paused struck me as though a switch had mentally clicked in her. You could almost see her weighing her options as she stared at me with her large brown eyes, and for a fraction of a second, I knew she was going to say no. Until she said yes.

She was so different than anyone else I've ever known. She's damaged, like me. The difference between us is that I care far less about what I've been through. I've never had anything to lose, but she seems to think differently.

I knew that I could fall in love with her from the moment I saw her. Something about her felt like it belonged to me. She was familiar, and if I believed in it, I would almost say that it was love.

At first sight.

## ❧ 9 ❧
## FALLING

# M aggie

I GOT TO THE LIBRARY FIFTEEN MINUTES EARLY AND waited, wondering if he would even bother to show or if I had imagined it all. I pulled nervously on my sweater until it was longer on one side than the other, and then I tried to scrunch it up again.

At exactly noon, he walked through the library doors and walked right toward me as though he knew exactly where I would be sitting.

I spent the entire study session trying to do everything but stare into his beautiful eyes. I kept my head down and my eyes on our books, but I could feel him watching me even when I was trying to show him something in one of his text-books. I knew he wasn't paying attention. He made it a point to pull his chair right next to mine, and our arms were often close enough to touch, our faces so painfully close. His hand brushed against mine when he would move it to inquire about something I had told him fifteen minutes before, causing an electricity to run through me making me jumpy. Between the constant smiling and awkward glances, I knew neither of us was really paying attention to what we were supposed to be studying. Both of us kept creating excuses to accidentally touch one another again.

We finally settled in and began to focus, in spite of the electricity flowing between us. We studied for a few hours until we reluctantly agreed we had made good progress and agreed to meet again the next day. After we had packed up our bags and slowly got ready to leave we lingered on the library steps.

"You did well," I said, smiling at him and trying not to think about how close he was standing to me, making it difficult to breathe.

"Thank you. Not too bad for someone stupid like me," Sam said, smiling crookedly.

"You're not stupid!" I said a little too forcefully, wondering why he would say something like that. He was smarter than he gave himself credit for, and I loved watching him grasp the things he struggled with. I stared at him hard, trying to make my words sink in. "You're not stupid."

"Thanks, but I know that I'm not that smart, at least not as smart as you are. I appreciate you helping me," Sam mumbled a little as he looked down at the ground for a moment.

"You're smarter than you think you are, Sam. I can tell." I willed him to look at me, and as though he'd heard my thoughts, he looked up.

"I like you, Mags," Sam said, shortening my name in a way that nobody else ever did and making my heart flutter. Nobody had ever given me a special name, and I liked the intimacy of knowing that he was the only one who had done that. To everyone else I was just Maggie, or to my mother, Margaret.

"I'd like to be friends and hang out, if that would be okay with you."

I paused. I hadn't had a friend since Trip, and I was unsure. Why would he want to be friends with me? A shudder ran through me as I reminded myself that it had been almost seven years since that horrible night with Trip.

I tried to tell myself that Sam was different. I had stayed away from men and women, keeping to myself as much as possible, afraid that someone would see how damaged I was, but something about Sam drew me in.

He was different.

"I don't know," I said, hesitantly. "I'm really busy."

"Oh, okay," he said, hurt resonating through his voice. "I know you must have better things to do than hang out with some idiot like me. I guess we can just stick to the tutoring."

"No ... I mean ... I don't really have a lot of friends," I said, afraid of his reaction as the words fell from my mouth. I knew that he must have a lot of friends and would instantly realize that I was a loser.

"I don't have a lot of friends, either. Not real ones anyway," he said wryly. He stared deeply into my eyes, making me squirm. "If you wanted, we could be friends."

My cheeks felt hot as I tried to catch my breath.

What if he found out about Trip and what happened to me? My stomach turned just thinking about it, my tongue tied as he looked at me, expecting a response.

"Think about it. I'll text you, if that's okay," he said finally, briefly touching my shoulder.

I nodded.

I hadn't had a friend for as long as I could remember, and as I watched him walk away, I fought the urge to follow after him. but I didn't.

I reminded myself that there was no way he would ever want to be with someone like me, who had been used and abused, then thrown away so heartlessly. I had been far stupider than anyone could ever imagine, and there was no way he would ever want to be with someone as pathetic as me.

❧

MAGGIE

AS SOON AS I GOT HOME FROM THE LIBRARY, ALMOST AS though he knew I had just walked in the door, he texted me.

"I liked spending time with you today."

I smiled, unsure if I had stopped since leaving him, a sensation like a warm blanket coming over me. "I liked it, too."

"So, I'll see you tomorrow?"

"Yes."

"How did your date go?" My mother was behind me, her voice making me jump. She asked innocently but pointedly.

"It wasn't a date," I sighed, hiding my phone.

"You sure took an awfully long time to get ready if it wasn't a date," she said, her deep brown eyes, exactly like mine, pressed into me the way they did when she wanted more than I wanted to give her.

"It wasn't a date," I repeated.

"Well that's good," she said her voice getting tight in the way that it did whenever she thought I was purposely being difficult with her. I usually was. "You weren't exactly dressed for a date, anyway."

I ran up to my room and closed the door, thankful for the solitude. My room was the one place in the house where my mother never seemed comfortable. It was the one area in which I had complete control, and the one place I knew I was safe from her.

My phone beeped. Sam!

"Can I see you? Now?"

"Now? You just saw me?" I flopped down on my bed in wonder. Why would he want to see me again today?

As if on cue, my phone beeped again.

"The truth is, I wanted to get to know you more today, but I chickened out because I thought it was too soon. I want to see you. Too soon?"

My heart started racing. The smile spread across my face, and I realized that I felt like the Cheshire Cat in *Alice in Wonderland*, one of my favorite childhood books.

I couldn't believe anybody would ever want to spend time with me. I was damaged and ruined, which I thought was obvious to everyone. How could Sam not see it? What could he possibly see in me when he had every beautiful girl on campus dying to spend time with him?

I was nothing compared to them, or him.

My mother's words always haunted me, and I became them, always trapped in a cycle of never being good enough. "Oh, Maggie, you would be so pretty if you could just lose that ten extra pounds you always seem to carry, or if you would just do something with your hair, but I guess you have to work with what God gave you, right?

My mother was beautiful and thin and perfect and always had been. Her mother had made sure of it, and my mother was trying to make sure that I was following in her footsteps. She had spent my entire life reminding me that I didn't quite live up to her expectations, which played in my head repeatedly as though it was Groundhog Day.

My phone beeped again, startling me out of my thoughts.

"Hey? R u there?"

"Sorry ... Where?" I was still smiling.

"Where? Where do I want to see you?"

"Yes. Where to meet?"

We agreed to meet at a local hangout, fifteen minutes from my house. The cautious side of me that usually took the lead began to creep in, but the little voice inside of my head told me that this was different than it had been with Trip. It told me that he was safe, and I listened to it because I wanted to.

I ran a brush through my hair and wondered for a brief moment if I should just message him back and tell him that I was tired and going to just crash for the night. *Is it weird that he wants to see me so soon after we just saw each other? Maybe there's something wrong with him ...*

I shook my head, remembering the way he had looked at me earlier, so deeply, as though he already knew me, something so strangely familiar in his gaze.

Nobody had ever looked into me the way that he did, and my stomach felt anxious just thinking about it. I smoothed back my hair with my hands, thinking for a brief moment that my mom was right and that I should do something with it. It was just a boring brown and dull, and always a bit unruly, no matter how much product I put in it. I contemplated changing my sweater, but after a few minutes of going back and forth, I decided to leave on what I was wearing. I didn't want to appear to be too high maintenance, which I wasn't at all. I snuck out the door without my mother seeing me, breathing a sigh of relief when I got to my car without having to answer a thousand questions.

She was notorious for her questions. "Where are you going? How long will you be gone? Have you been there before? How do you know he's not a serial killer? Are you going to eat? Is the food good there? Do they have any healthy options? Will you be drinking? Should we wait up for you?"

I walked into the bar, nearly giddy with my ability to escape undetected. I spotted him immediately sitting on a bar stool with an empty one right next to him. He broke into a huge smile and motioned for me to come over.

"Hey," he said when I sat down.

"Hi."

"I'm glad you came out. I knew it was a risk asking because you might think I was a crazy serial killer or something, but I swear I'm not. I just wanted to see you again, and I didn't want to wait." He stared into me the way that he had earlier, and I was blinded by nothing but blue.

We sat for a few hours talking about everything and nothing, tuning out the music and the noise around us. I could hear nothing but the sound of his beautifully deep, perfect voice, and there was nothing but him, right in front of me, leaning into me and hanging on to every word I said as though I was the most important person in the world.

I felt as though I had known him my entire life, a strange familiarity creeping in to every moment I spent with him. I was afraid and cautious of everyone I had ever met, but Sam was different. Sam felt like home, and even though the thought of him sent butterflies through my stomach and chest, being with him gave me a calm that I'd never had with anyone else my entire life.

Sam didn't make me feel self-conscious as he listened to me, and for some reason I knew that with him I was safe. Talking to him made me feel as though we had been talking our entire lives. He listened with an intensity that made me feel as though he was truly interested, and when he spoke, I closed my eyes, his deep timber voice seeping into my soul and becoming a part of me.

Within a few short hours we were holding hands, our

fingers electric, connecting us together, and I felt as though we were always meant to be together.

All at once I felt as though something inside of me was changing, forever.

As we talked, I realized we had always been one moment away from one another all our lives. There were too many things that drew us together, too may coincidences. Our families grew up one town away from one another, and we knew a lot of the same people but had never actually met.

We both had a strange affinity for black licorice but hated chocolate, and as the night wore on, we found that we could practically finish one other's sentences. There was an incredibly intense chemistry between us, an unseen thread that drew us toward each another without resistance as though we were two missing pieces finding one another for the first time. We were connected, and I found it hard to believe that I had ever lived my life without him, all memories fading into the background as he became everything that had ever mattered.

He made every excuse to touch me and play with my hair, and I made sure that I took every opportunity to lean into him, breathing in his scent, absorbing his words so I could play them over in my head when I was home alone.

"Do you feel..." he said as he pushed an unruly curl behind my ear.

"Yes," I breathed, his touch electrifying.

"I just wanted to make sure I wasn't the only one. It's like we've known each other longer than this life. It's like I've always known you," he said, not breaking eye contact as I sat mesmerized.

"Yes," I breathed. "You make me feel so much different than anyone ever has in my entire life. You make me feel ... free."

He smiled when I spoke as though I was the most important person in the world, his eyes glued to my lips.

"I want to kiss you," he said, his face only inches from mine.

"Oh my," I said, his words making my stomach flip.

"Can I?"

I stared into his eyes as I let my tongue dart over my lips, wetting them just enough. "Please."

In a moment, his lips were on mine, soft but wanting, unlike anything I had ever experienced in my entire life. Warmth travelled through my entire body as my hands found his face, his fingers buried in my hair.

Time stood completely still, and just as he pulled away, I was aware that I couldn't breathe. My entire body was on high alert, on a different level of awareness than it had ever been. I willed myself to breathe. As we stared at one another, I saw a look in his eyes that filled me with want.

I felt something inside of me click, like the last piece of a puzzle had been inserted in place, the moment between us completely frozen, and I knew that there was absolutely no turning back. I was his, and he was mine, and there was nothing that I could, or even wanted, to do about it.

I was falling, and I understood from the moment I laid eyes on him that there had never been another choice.

He had never been a choice, and nothing could've stopped me from falling in love with him even if I tried.

## 10

# SAVE ME

M aggie

OUR LOVE CAME QUICKLY.

It was idyllic and perfect, and if I had been in my right mind, I would've known not to trust it because trusting was dangerous. I didn't know that I was lost, but I knew I would fall in love him the moment he kissed me that night at the bar. His lips were soft and wet, leaving me dizzy and wanting his fingers hot on my skin.

The first kiss and every kiss after left me completely breathless inside and out. It was the kind that when I thought about it years later, my lips still remembered the tingle all the way to the tips of my toes, and I could remember nothing ever being so delicious.

After our first date together, we were together as much as possible.

"I have to be with you as much as I can." Sam understood

the sweetness of a kiss, or the softness of a touch. He enjoyed the experience of simply drinking in the smell of one another, and when we lay on his bed, our eyes locked onto one another's, time stood still. His hands always seemed to find mine, his fingers either roaming down my back or sides, his touch electrifying me even through my clothes. I reveled in his need to touch me, and I did the same, touching his shoulders, back, or hands every chance I got, just to remind myself that he was real and that this wasn't all a dream.

I was undeniably attracted to him, yet I tried to remain cautious until it became clear to me that his main objective wasn't to get me into bed. He didn't care if we took things slow and never tried to push. My guard was beginning to come down slowly, though not completely. With him, I felt safer than I ever had with anyone else.

The memory of Trip was beginning to fade, and I no longer cringed at human contact. Sam's touch healed me from the disgust I had felt for as long as I could remember. I had never allowed another person to touch me, always pulling away as though their imprint might burn my skin. When there was accidental contact I couldn't help but stiffen and pull away, my body responding with disgust.

Sam's touch was different, but every now and again I was catapulted back to that moment in time when my face was shoved into the pillow with Trip grunting above me, telling me to relax, and in that moment I would freeze.

The moments when I pulled away from Sam were fewer and farther between, but when it happened, he gave me the space I needed, not questioning until it couldn't be avoided any longer.

"You pull away..." he said, a question in his blue eyes.

"Yes," I said, burying my head into his shoulder, his arms automatically tightening their hold on me. "I can't help it."

He was silent, until his deep voice sounded gently in my ear. "You were hurt?"

"Yes," I said, my voice barely audible.

"When?"

"In high school," I said trying to get the words out. I had never talked about it before and doing so was more difficult than I imagined.

"By a man?" His breathing was beginning to come faster as he got more upset.

"No." I said, my voice cracking. "By a boy."

Sam's body tightened, and I could feel his jaw clench above me as he held me in silence.

"Were you ... hurt bad?" His words were slow, and I could tell he was afraid of the answer.

"No ... not too badly, but it made me afraid," I admitted. "It was only once."

He breathed out.

"I would never hurt you." His voice was ragged, and I could hear the pain in it. "I'll always protect you, Mags. I'm so sorry that it happened ... to you. I would kill anyone who ever tried to hurt you. Nobody will ever hurt you ever again."

"I know you would ever hurt me," I said, feeling the weight of my admission lift from my shoulders. "Thank you for taking care of me."

"I'll always take care of you. Always."

I was relieved that he didn't ask me for details. I didn't want to tell him everything that happened that awful night. I knew that he would just know that it was terrible, and he wouldn't make me relive the horror and humiliation.

It was as though he had been made to love me, and finally the world, and my existence in it, made perfect sense.

AFTER A MONTH WE WERE COMPLETELY INSEPARABLE, AND I had practically moved into his apartment. I met his mom, Julie, and he met my parents, who were less than impressed with him, especially my mother.

My father only ever seemed to be along for the ride, and as much as I adored him, I wished he would find his voice every now and again and speak up. He had always been soft spoken, and it was understood that my mother was the one in charge, but he seemed to have no heart, and I'd wondered my entire life how he had become this way. The older I grew, the less of a man he seemed to become as I witnessed his slow but steady emasculation. It made me sad for him, though I had never been Daddy's Little Girl, preferring to be on my own more than attached to two parents that I never felt I belonged to.

As I was packing up some of my things to take over to Sam's apartment, my mother walked gingerly into my bedroom. I watched, amused, as she seemed to be testing for roadside bombs with each tiny step. For some reason she had never been comfortable in my room, and we had an unspoken rule early on that she didn't belong there.

"There is something about him that I just don't trust, Margaret. You're moving way too fast for a girl who has had no experience with boys or men." She tried to perch herself awkwardly on my bed as I tried to hide my amusement at her effort to seem comfortable when she clearly wasn't. "Let's face it, it's not as though you're the kind of girl that guys fall all over themselves to get."

I ignored the sting of her words, as I had long since trained myself to do. "Mother, everything is going to work out just fine. He's not a serial killer or an idiot, he's ... everything."

"All I'm saying, Margaret, is that you're very inexperienced and you don't know anything about him. You're moving entirely too quickly for my liking."

"Well, it's a good thing *you're* not going out with him, now isn't it?" I could feel my anger reaching the surface as my voice started to rise.

Her eyes darkened as she opened her mouth to say something, and then changed her mind.

I went back to packing, ignoring her until she finally retreated, her attempt at giving me motherly advice thwarted.

Sam had been less than impressed with her as well. "Your mom looks a lot like you, and is pretty good looking for her age, Mags. But what's with the stick up her ass? You two are night and day."

I knew these weren't the kinds of relationships that would resolve themselves overnight, so I decided to give it some time. After all, we *were* moving quickly, and my mother wasn't completely wrong to be wary of him. But I knew this was the kind of love you find once in a lifetime, and I wasn't going to give that up for anyone.

When Sam looked at me, I could tell by the look in his eyes that he truly saw *me*. I don't know how or why he found me, but I was so thankful he did. My entire life I had gone unseen by the people who were supposed to love me the most, but when he looked at me, I knew that had changed.

I had never been that drawn to another human being in my entire life, almost like a giant magnet was placed right in the center of me, pulling me toward him in a way I couldn't control.

For the first time that I could ever remember I was happy and so was he, always laughing and smiling whenever we were together and sullen when we weren't. He texted me from classes to let me know he was missing me, which I encouraged him to stop doing if he wanted to pass.

After a few months, his grades were finally improving, and

he was no longer in jeopardy of failing. When our grades came in the mail, he flew into the bedroom where I had been lounging on a lazy Saturday.

"I'm passing, Mags! I'm actually going to make it through this semester!" Sam jumped on the bed, ecstatic with the news. He grabbed and hugged me, pressing me against his lean muscular frame. I melted into him, marveling at how being near him never got old. "I'm going to pass my classes thanks to you!"

Happiness bubbled up inside of me. "It's because of you, not because of me, Sam. You're smarter than you realize."

"No, I'm not. I'm not smart. The only smart thing I ever did was to ask you to help me. Otherwise, I would have just drunk myself out of school." Sam's blue eyes were dark. "You saved me."

He trailed his fingers down my cheek gently as he often did, but his time it was different. Even though we'd lived together for several months, we had taken it slow. This time when he touched me, the look in his eyes was different, and I felt a pull deep in the center of me that I'd never experienced before.

"What did I save you from?" I asked, my breath catching in my chest as I moved closer to him.

"Myself," he said lying back on the bed and pulling me close. "You saved me from myself."

"What does that mean?" I asked, curious about the sadness that lay behind his eyes.

"Nothing," he smiled, kissing me over and over on the lips until I no longer remembered the question. I opened my body and soul up to him for the first time, trusting him with every part of my being, our bodies entwined and discovering each other in every possible away.

I trusted him with every fiber of my being, and when he claimed me as his own, I thought of nothing else, my mind blessedly and deliciously full of nothing but Sam, and I knew that finally I was free.

THE NEXT COUPLE OF YEARS WENT BY QUICKLY AS WE worked and studied, pushing each other to get through school. We reveled in our togetherness, shutting out the rest of the world to live in our own private cocoon.

The only other person we allowed in was Sam's mom, Julie.

Julie was the perfect combination of warm and sweet, like apple pie with cinnamon served right out of the oven and topped off with vanilla bean ice cream. She had been broken, cheated on, abandoned by her husband and left with nearly nothing. But she was strong and good, and no matter what she experienced, she tried to find something she could learn from it. She was like a mom to me, her eyes as blue as Sam's when his were blue, her smile exactly the same. We went to her house often, and I always felt welcome. Sam and his mom laughed. A lot. Their entire lives had revolved around one another, and they shared jokes and conversations that I often didn't understand, but I didn't ask about them because it made me happy to see their happiness.

Even though there had been a lot more struggle in their lives and a lot less to be happy about at times, they tried to find the good in things. Their lives had been so different than mine, yet I was jealous of their optimism and their closeness. I had grown up with two parents, but I would have preferred to be with Sam and Julie over them anytime. Julie was unlike my own mother, who could easily suck the fun out of anything and everything, and my father who stood by, silently, and allowed her to do it.

Somehow, Julie and Sam had figured out how to find the

silver lining in every cloud, no matter how hard they had to look for it. Julie said Sam taught her how to do that from the moment he was born, and he said she taught him.

Julie was grateful to me for loving her son, and while I thought she might resent me for taking him away from her, she seemed to love me all the more for being so good to him. But most of all, she was grateful that I pushed him to get through school. She didn't want him to work as a waiter for the rest of his life, though he was good at it, and the money paid for a lot of his education. But she'd waited tables all her life, raising Sam on her own. She didn't want his life to be as hard as hers had been. She wanted his life to be different and "to matter," she always said.

I even planned to go to graduation with Julie and Sam. I wanted to enjoy the day, though I dreaded telling my mother that I wouldn't be spending the entire day with her and my dad. As I always did, when I was preparing to tell my mother something I knew she wouldn't like, I waited until the last minute. I knew that she would at least appreciate it if I told them in person, so I went to my parent's house the morning of the ceremony.

"I'm going to graduation with the Connors," I blurted out, almost as soon as I walked in the door.

My mother ignored me, like she often did when I was telling her something she didn't want to hear.

"I have everything planned for your graduation party, which I've put a lot of work into," she said, straightening flowers in an arrangement she was working on, refusing to look at me.

"Thank you, Mother. Did you hear what I said?"

"Yes. I heard what you said. Even though your father and I paid for your college, your books, and all your other expenses, you are going to graduation with the Connors."

Mother continued to look down and busy herself with her flowers.

"It's not that. It's just that Sam is my life, and I want to spend the day with him." I was trying to sound convincing, but I felt myself caving in to her disapproval as I had all of my life.

"Well, how will it look when we all show up separately?"

It would have been so much easier if we could all go together. But Sam and I had tried to have the parents spend time together a couple of times during holidays and birthdays, all with the same result. The first time my mother met Julie she said with thinly veiled disdain, "Oh ... so you're a waitress? Didn't you ever want to go to college and get a real job?"

We didn't encourage them getting together much.

Julie Connors had been a good mom, but she had done everything on her own. Sam was a 'mistake', and she had been young. We were already half her age, and she was younger than most of our friends' parents by a good five to ten years. Still in great shape, she was sober and grounded. Her only vices were cigarettes and coffee. She had been forced to be strong all her life because her mom died when she was five and her dad when she was twenty. Julie had been married at eighteen, pregnant, and had barely finished high school. At twenty-one her marriage was annulled, and that was the last time she saw her husband. There was nothing that she and my mother had in common, and my mother's outward disdain for Julie prevented them from ever having a relationship of any kind.

All my life, my mother cared more about appearances and less about love, and being a mother hadn't changed any of that for her.

"I don't care ..." I started to argue with her.

My father simply said, "Let her go with the boy, Diane.

We'll see her there." Then he gave me an uncharacteristic wink, which made me love him all the more, though I was sorry for the sadness in his life. My mother was critical with me, but was even more so with him, and I wondered for the thousandth time how he could stand it.

I raced back to our apartment so I get could dressed, excited for our big graduation day. As I was finishing I felt something sharp in the edge of the cap. I looked at Sam, who smiled mischievously. When I finally found the ring, pulling it slowly out of a tiny gap in the edging of the cap, I turned around to find Sam down on one knee. All six feet and two inches of him was kneeling right in front of me. His eyes were aqua that day, ever changing, ever beautiful.

"I love you Mags, so much more than I ever expected to when I met you five years ago. More than I ever thought I could ever love anyone. If it weren't for you, I wouldn't even be graduating today. You grounded me and helped me see what was important. I know I would've lost my way without you there to steady me, and I can't imagine spending my life with anyone else but you. There is something about you that makes me want to be a better man, and maybe even a father someday, which is nothing I ever thought I would want to be." He ran his fingers through his thick hair and smiled that goofy grin that made me want to grab him and kiss him hard. "Will you marry me, Mags?"

I stared at him for a moment. The lumberjack beard that he had been growing wasn't working for me, but his eyes spoke to me, shined for me, and saying 'No' was not an option. I jumped at him and he caught me, rather awkwardly. I kissed his face until we were both laughing so hard with tears streaming down our faces, and in that moment, I knew there would never be another love for me.

"Is that a 'yes'?" he asked when we finally stood up, trying to get a hold of ourselves.

"Yes!" I said, allowing him to slip the sparkling ring on my finger, admiring his choice. "You shouldn't have, Sam. This must have cost..."

"Don't worry about what it cost!" he scolded, grabbing me and holding tight. "You are worth it, and when I have more money I will get you a bigger ring. Nothing will ever be good enough for you, Mags. And I'll take good care of you. We'll get married and buy a house and have an incredible life. A normal life, and a good life. It'll be a life that neither one of ever had, but we'll make it what we always wanted it to be."

And when I looked at him, I allowed myself to believe for the first time that we could be truly happy together, and then I cried.

I cried because I knew how hard it was for him to say those things. He had never even allowed himself to want those things until now. Until us. And I loved him for trusting us so much that he let himself envision a future where he could finally be happy.

A future with me.

**❧**

SAM

I laid next to her and watched her sleep, the excitement from the day wearing us both out.

I always felt like a creeper when I watched her sleep, but I needed to remind myself that she was here and real. Her beautiful face against the pillow looking so peaceful gives me hope. When I brush her dark curls away from her cheeks, my fingers grazing her skin lightly, I want to believe that it'll always be this perfect. When she nuzzles her face against my chest, sighing in her sleep and smiling as though she's the happiest person in the world, my heart fills up to nearly bursting, and I want to hold onto the moment forever.

It's a ritual to stare at her almost every night and watch her sleep, convincing myself that I deserve her even though deep down I know that I don't.

I don't ever sleep much and never have, trying to fend off the demons and the memories that never leave me alone for too long. I want to forget and be an entirely different person, but I've seen too much and know too much about how shitty this life can be.

But, I've found her so now I lie awake and wonder how I got so damned lucky to have someone like Mags love me as much as she does. When she looks up at me with those smoky dark eyes, I just want to hold onto her forever and never let go. It crushes me to imagine ever losing her, even though I wait for it to happen.

I know that one day it will, even though I hold onto the hope that it'll always be this way, but I know that she'll realize who and what I am, and eventually she'll leave me. She'll hate me for not telling her the truth, and she'll walk away, disgusted. I don't know if my heart will be able to take it.

I'd never felt so connected to anyone, even though I'd tried, but none of the girls I've ever met have ever compared to her.

Mom always tells me that I'm crazy and that I deserve a chance at happiness, but even she doesn't know. She wants to believe the best in me, but she doesn't know who I really am.

I told myself I'd never buy a girl a ring, but I saved and saved, and when I saw that pile of money in my account, I knew what I'd been saving for. Even when I bought it, imagining it on her finger, I couldn't believe I was doing it. I tried to convince myself that even though I gave it to her, I'd never go through with it because in the end I'll only hurt her.

I can't stand the thought of her hating me, but once she truly knows me, she will. I don't know if I can live if she does. I remind myself that if I truly ever loved her that I would let her go. I would walk away from her and let her be free, because in the end I'll only break her heart, and she'll break mine.

There are too many things she doesn't know, and I want to keep it that way. I want to make sure that she never has to look at me with disappointment or shame and that she'll always love me.

But I've seen too much to know that it won't end well for either of us, and I hate myself for getting in this deep.

## ❧  II  ☙

## GRADUATING LIFE

A s we stood in Julie's living room getting ready to leave for graduation, she snapped picture after picture on her phone, with her camera, one after another after another.

"I'm sorry for all the pictures," she said, crying and laughing all at once, her makeup running for the third time. "I'm just so proud of Sam. And you too, of course, sweetie." when her makeup ran off, she looked younger. I thought she was beautiful, and I could tell Sam did, too. He smiled at her warmly, and as he did so, I realized that I couldn't recall a time when he had ever been upset with her. He loved her and protected her, and she could do no wrong in his eyes

"Mom, we have to go or we're going to be late," Sam smiled as he said it.

"Oh, yes, you can't be late!" she said, gathering her things together frantically, her hands shaking. "I'm just so nervous. You would think it was me going up there to graduate."

"Mom," Sam grabbed her hands and held them tight. "It is you going up there. It's still you and me, don't forget."

"Yes, you and me," she said, tears shining in her eyes.

It had always been Julie and Sam, mom and son. It had never been another way. They were close, protective of one another, yet nurturing at the same time.

"I hate to break this party up, but neither of us are going to walk if we don't leave now." I looked at my phone nervously.

"Oh no, we don't want that. Let's go." Julie grabbed her camera, purse, phone, camera bag and make up and raced to the car. I volunteered to drive so Julie could do her make up.

"I'm sorry, I'm sorry," she said as she put on her eye shadow, her hands still quivering.

"It's okay!" I said, glancing at her in the rearview mirror. "Sam probably would have made us late anyway."

"Ha!" he said, pretending to take a whack at me.

"The ring!" she said, suddenly.

"What ring?" Sam asked innocently.

"Oh my God, I was so busy having a nervous breakdown I didn't ask you if she said 'yes'!" Julie started crying again. "Oh Lord, I don't know what is wrong with me. I can't stop crying today. I'm sorry."

"Of course she said 'yes'! Who wouldn't say 'yes' to me?" Sam joked.

"It's okay, Julie. Don't worry about it!" I was grinning from ear to ear. Every time I moved my hand, it sparkled in the sunlight. I loved how it looked on my finger, and I couldn't wait to show it off. I thought about my parents and knew they wouldn't love it, but I didn't care. Their disapproval no longer paralyzed me like it once did, and for the first time that I could remember, I felt free.

"I'm so happy for you two kiddos!" Julie gushed. Her face suddenly fell. "What are your parents going to say?"

"It's my life. They'll just have to deal with it." I smiled as I said it. I hadn't stopped smiling since Sam slipped the ring on my finger, and I knew there was no way I was going to stop smiling. Life was beautiful and gorgeous and perfect. Happy. And nothing was going to ruin it.

We pulled into the parking lot and got out of the car. Sam grabbed my hand, and we walked into the auditorium, ready to face our future, together.

## ❧ 12 ❧

# THE BEGINNING OF THE END

M aggie

AFTER GRADUATION, TIME FLEW BY QUICKLY. WE PUT OUT resumés and searched on line for jobs.

As predicted, my parents weren't thrilled by our engagement. My mother made some backhanded comment about how he was "supposed to use a certain amount of his salary to buy the ring," but we anticipated it and ignored her. My father looked worried, but he smiled anyway and congratulated us.

We thought about buying a house but didn't have the money or credit, so we rented a bigger apartment close to his mom. I liked that Sam wanted to look out for her. His friends had been teasing him all his life for being a 'Mama's boy,' but he shrugged it off. He didn't care what they thought. His mom had taken care of him, raising him to be the man he had become, and they still needed one another. He never apologized to anyone for that.

We interviewed for jobs. We wagered who would get one first. The loser had to cook dinner for the other.

Naked.

He lost.

I was hired almost immediately to be a teacher at a center for disabled children. It was a difficult job, but one I had been well prepared for. I loved my job even though the hours were full and long, and the strain of it exhausted me, but I loved the children. Making an impact in their lives was far more than I had ever imagined.

With Sam losing his bet, he finally conceded and cooked dinner for me, although I could tell he wasn't terribly thrilled about it.

"I'm going to end up catching my boys on fire, Mags. Then you'll really be sorry!" he said half-serious and half-joking.

"Your 'boys' will be covered up with an apron so stop trying to get out of it!" I kissed him long and hard to distract him, which always seemed to work. He had no idea how much I had been looking forward to watching him cook in nothing but an apron. He had finally cut his beard down so he looked like a sexy mountain man instead of a gnarly lumberjack. Regardless, I got to sit at the kitchen table and watch him cook dinner while staring at his beautiful perfect ass at the same time.

At some point, I made him take the apron off and even elected to help him with my teeth. We got distracted and forgot to turn the stove off as we satisfied our burning need for one another, which resulted in him also horribly burning dinner.

Finally sated and hungry, we ordered out that night and had a perfect dinner of sesame chicken and egg rolls on paper plates. We drank cheap wine out of red solo cups, and I couldn't recall ever being happier.

We made sure to christen all five rooms in the new apartment, our bodies fitting together like a perfect puzzle, our hunger for one another ever present. We were drawn together by a touch or a glance, sometimes for long passionate hours, and other times for quick, raucous, porn sex that left us both panting, aching, and wanting more. Sam had a way of igniting my want so that I was practically climbing on top of him every chance I got. He loved making me want him so much with little more than a light touch or a flick of his tongue, and I loved that he could do that to me.

We anticipated that he would get a job or an internship any day. He was an artist at heart, but a graphic designer by trade. His work and his pieces were good, but the design skills on his resume were what would end up paying the bills. He had always been an artist, sketching, doodling, and drawing. It had been his outlet when he was young, and he'd honed his passion all of his life.

In our spare time he painted and I wrote poetry. We realized that our artistic hearts were yet another thing that drew our souls so deeply and hopelessly together, and we loved each other even more for it.

WHEN JULIE CALLED TWO MONTHS LATER WHILE I WAS preparing dinner and waiting for Sam to come home from a third and final job interview, I could barely understand her. The sounds coming from the other end of the phone sounded more like a wounded animal than the woman I had come to love like a mother.

"Mags! Come. Now ... Now!" the voice on the other end

was crying hysterically, I could hardly make out any of the words she was saying.

"Julie, what is it? Where are you?"

"Come now. You have to come!"

"Where?"

"Hospital."

My heart stopped beating, though I could hear the blood pounding in my ears. My face was hot. "Why? Who is in the hospital?"

"Sam."

"Oh, God."

"Mags, come now!"

I don't even know how I made it to the hospital, the drive like a bad dream. My hands were shaking as I tried my best to breathe. My chest was pounding as though my heart would explode out of it and all over the steering wheel.

I kept telling myself to stay calm. Stay calm. Stay calm. Stay calm. Stay calm. Everything is going to be okay. Stay calm. Stay calm. Stay calm. Don't freak out. Stay calm.

Every red light made me want to jump out of my skin. The twenty-minute drive to the hospital felt like an eternity as I sped up to sixty miles per hour on every street until I finally jumped the curb to get into the hospital parking lot.

Emergency room. Emergency room. Stay calm, Mags. Don't freak out.

I ran into the lobby, the doors almost not opening fast enough as I nearly slammed right into them. I pushed my way through, angrily.

"Can I help you?" there was a nurse in triage.

"Samuel Connors. I'm here for Samuel Connors." I was trembling, and I could barely catch my breath. The nurse was moving too slowly. "I'm here for Samuel Connors."

"Yes, hold on. I'm looking for him now." She was staring at a monitor, her eyes darting back and forth, revealing nothing. Giving away nothing. I waited for her to gasp or to scream when she found his name, but she simply looked at me and said "Bed three, but they are moving him to the ICU very shortly."

ICU? ICU? Intensive Care Unit? Oh, God.

She pointed me in the right direction and swiped her card so the doors would open. I walked frantically through the square cube that the ER was set up in, looking for bed three...

Bed three!

I took a deep breath and pushed the curtain back. When I saw him I suddenly felt dizzy as a feeling of sheer terror filled me from the inside out, and I nearly fainted.

## ❦ 13 ❦

# LUMBERJACK

M aggie

"MAGS, THANK GOD YOU'RE HERE!" JULIE GRASPED MY arm, holding me up. I could feel the blood rushing from my face, my legs weak. I needed to sit but I couldn't. All I could do was stare.

I stared down at Sam, his face swollen and full of cuts and dried up blood. His eyes were closed, and all I could see was black and blue. His hands and arms still had crusted blood on them, and his arms were full of tubes and IVs, beeping monitors everywhere with tubes coming out of his nose and mouth.

"Sam? Oh, God, Sam?" my voice was small and barely audible. "Sam? Are you in there?"

Suddenly a beeping sound came from one of the machines and it was flashing red. A flurry of activity entered the room, and we were ushered out quickly before we even knew what was happening. A nurse with a stern face directed us to follow her into the hall where she led us to a family lounge. It was decorated to look like someone's living room, but I knew it was just a room where you waited for bad news. There were boxes of tissues everywhere, and the faint smell of chemicals burned into my nose.

"Someone will come in for you when he is stable," the nurse who said. Her voice was curt as her eyes avoided ours.

I was too stunned to talk or to even breathe. I was afraid to move.

"Are you okay, sweetie?" Julie asked in between sobs.

"I don't know. I don't know if I'm okay. What's happening? What in the hell is going on?" I was lost.

"I don't know. All I know is that he was hit by someone while driving home. The driver was going in the wrong direction. I don't know anything other than that." Julie looked how I felt; stunned, as though her entire world had been ripped apart in front of her.

"W-w-why didn't anyone call me?" I asked. It suddenly occurred to me that I was the last to know.

"I guess I'm still listed as his 'In case of emergency'," Julie said carefully, tears still streaming down her face.

"Oh," was all I could think of to respond.

The next few hours were a blur as we sat in the lounge waiting for news. A doctor finally came in a few hours later, and in my daze, I could pick out words like "trauma, coma, swollen brain, wait and see," while Julie focused and had the real conversations. Suddenly, I felt like a child, young, ridiculous, and completely useless in my plight. There was nothing I could say or do, nothing I could ask or contribute. I just sat and stared and let Julie handle the difficult stuff. I let her do the heavy lifting while I lost myself in my shock and fear.

The doctor was kind as he spoke to both of us.

Kindness was good. Kindness was reassuring, this much I did know.

The doctor finally left, and I turned and glanced at Julie who looked like she had just been hit by a car or two.

"Are you okay, Mags?" Julie asked, putting her hand gently on my head.

I nodded, feeling numb. "Is he going to ... to ... "

"No! God no!" Julie said a little too loudly. Julie's voice broke as she said the words. "You heard him sweetie, it's just too soon to tell."

We sat in silence holding one another. The room around us still as we worked hard to breathe. It felt as though all the air had been sucked out of the room as I gasped for breath, fighting the dizziness that threatened to overtake me. Our entire world was lying in that room, filled with tubes and wires that neither of us could comprehend. A world without Sam was unthinkable and impossible.

"What do we do? Can we stay here until he wakes up?" I couldn't bear the thought of going back to our apartment and him not being there.

"The doctor said we can stay here if we want." Julie was trying to stay strong for me, but I could tell it was getting harder and harder. "I'm not planning on leaving, Mags."

I nodded. I knew that neither of us could bear the thought of leaving Sam alone.

❦

IT WAS THE THIRD NIGHT IN THE HOSPITAL, AND I WAS dreaming.

I knew I was dreaming, but it was the type of dream you don't want to wake up from. Sam was kissing me, softly. The kind of kiss I loved the most. He was teasing me with his lips and his tongue, nibbling on my lips gently. I could feel my body waking up to him, coming alive as I moved toward him, trying to get as close as I could, trying to wrap his body around mine.

But suddenly he stopped kissing me, and he began to move farther away, slowly at first, but then faster. I ran toward him, and the harder I ran, the further he got until he became a distant shadow, and I was crying from my effort to catch him ... crying out his name, still feeling his teeth on my lips, his breath on me.

Suddenly I was shaking, hard.

"Mags! Mags! Wake up!" Julie was calling out to me, and she continued to shake me. "You're dreaming."

I woke up with tears running down my face. It took me a moment to realize where I was, but when I moved my stiff neck, I remembered that I was lying on the couch in the family lounge.

It had been days, and there was still no change. Sam stubbornly remained in his coma, and Julie and I had yet to leave the hospital, sleeping off and on, taking turns sitting in the room with him while we waited for any sign of life.

"I'm going to go back into the room," I said, getting up and trying to stretch, happy to at least be in clean clothes and underwear.

My mother had been in one of her rare mothering moods and had agreed to bring me clothes, but had refused to stay.

"I feel like I'm intruding," she said in her typical tone that said she wanted to be invited to stay, but didn't really want to be there.

"No, mother, you're welcome to stay. Sam would be happy to know you were here," I lied.

She looked at me, her brown eyes dark, and for a moment I thought I saw something that resembled love or compassion reflecting in them. "No, I'm going to leave. Hospitals really aren't my thing. But here are your clothes. I tried to find something other than jeans or yoga pants, and I was careful not to make a mess of your apartment. Since it's already a wreck I don't suppose it would matter even if I did." With that, she kissed me on the cheek and walked out, leaving me to fend for myself emotionally as she had all of my life.

I had come to expect it, and deep down I knew that Sam would kill me if the first thing he woke up to was my mother. "She's mean in the worst way," he would tell me. He hated the compliments that were really meant to be insults, and the passive-aggressive approach she took with everyone. She commented about everything as though she was an authority on it and got offended if her words weren't taken as truth. I had grown up with her my entire life and was accustomed to having her hurt my feelings at a minimum of once a day, so I did my best to block her out. But Sam hadn't built up a resistance to her yet, and she drove him crazy.

He was used to Julie's transparency, and my mother was a much more difficult and exhausting pill to swallow. Deep down I knew that her leaving was a good thing, but a part of me still wished that I had a mother who could just comfort me.

I shook my head trying to regroup for a moment and walked quietly into his room. I looked at him, my beautiful man. His bruising and swelling were going down, and his face finally looked recognizable again. In his slumber, he at least looked peaceful.

"I'm here, my sweet lumberjack," I said, trying to make my voice sound as normal as possible. Since he had grown his beard, 'lumberjack' had become his new moniker. I didn't love the beard at first, but it was growing on me, and I realized that I would love him beard or no beard, hair or no hair. It didn't matter to me. I just loved him. "It's time to wake up now and talk to me, Sam. Did you have a good sleep?"

My question was met with nothing but the whistling and whirring of the machines.

"Wake up, Sam! Wake up! I had the weirdest dream about you," I said, grabbing his hand and stroking it. "It was a little naughty ..."

I thought that might get his attention, but he lay still as he had been for the past couple of days. I sat for a long time stroking his hand, enjoying the feel of his skin against mine. My soft hands against his manlier hands were such a contrast, and one I always enjoyed experiencing. I stopped myself as I started to think of my dream and his hands on my body. I didn't know when I would feel them again, and thinking of them at a time like this one just seemed wrong.

"The thing is, Sam, you have to come back to us. You have to wake up. Your mom needs you. I need you. Neither of us will know how to live without you. And you promised me a life that you can't go back on now. You are supposed to be my husband. We are going to have these amazing little beautiful babies, but first, you have to wake up. You have to come back to me." I laid my forehead on our entwined hands. "My life was nothing until I met you, and there is nothing I wouldn't do for you. I don't care if you're not exactly like you were. I'll be with you, every step of the way. I won't leave you. You'll always be 'my Sam.'"

The room was quiet. It was as though I was becoming immune to the noises of the hospital room in the short time I had been there, no longer hearing the beeping and buzzing. All I listened for was any sign or sound of Sam. But the constant sight of the tube down his throat to help him breathe always brought me back to reality.

I looked up at his scruffy face and his hair that I had combed back a few hours before. "God, you need a haircut, baby, so bad."

I thought about the first moment I saw him and the first

moment I knew I truly loved him. I thought about how much I needed him, how he had become such a part of me, and that I no longer knew how to breathe without him. When he wasn't with me, all I could think about was when he would be. He had ruined being alone for me, and I knew that I could never be without him again.

I kept my head down placing his fingers on my cheek. They were cold like his hands were, and I hoped the warmth from my cheek would warm them up. I focused all my thoughts on his fingertips and how they felt on my skin and on my face.

"You have to come back to me because I need you." I repeated over and over, tears running down my cheeks onto his fingertips. And as I closed my eyes, I thought that if he died, I would have to die, too, because there would be no reason to live without him.

## ❧ 14 ❧

## SINS OF THE FATHER

M aggie

I CLOSED MY EYES AND FELL ASLEEP. WHEN I AWOKE, I FELT like I had been sleeping for hours, and I realized the room was dark and completely silent.

Too dark. Too quiet.

There were no fluorescent lights, no whooshing of the ventilator or beeping of the IV machines. There was no silent chatter from the nurse's station or muted rings of the telephones. The hushed voices of family and hospital personnel was nonexistent.

There was nothing.

I stood up and turned around, first one way and then the other, searching for signs of anyone. Anywhere.

"Julie? Sam?" I called out, but my voice was silent. I felt myself call out, but there was no sound. Nothing. I tried again, "Julie! Sam!"

I walked around in blank space. There was no up or down, right or left, side to side. There was nothing but blankness. Nothing but nothingness.

Am I dreaming? I must be dreaming.

I tried to wake myself up. <u>Nothing.</u> I pinched myself as hard as I could. No pain.

I pinched myself again. Nothing. How is this possible?

"The mind is a powerful thing," Sam's voice reverberated through my head, and I realized at the same time that I wasn't really hearing him. Perhaps I was simply imagining him?

I turned and suddenly, he was there.

Sam. Sam. Where are you?

"I'm with you," Sam was being vague.

How are you with me? I don't know where you are. I don't know where I am! Where in the hell are we?

"I don't know, Mags. All I know is that you're here, with me." Sam sounded happy that I was here, though I still had no idea where here was. It was dark and strange, and I rubbed my eyes trying to bring everything into focus, but it didn't work. I felt disoriented as I slapped myself in the face trying to wake up.

Sam!

All at once, a little boy appeared in front of me. A little boy with bright blue eyes and thick brown hair, and I recognized him immediately. Sam!

"Mags!" Sam's voice echoed in my mind, though the little boy's lips didn't move.

Sam?

"I'm Sam." The little boy moved closer to me, and I could see my Sam in him. Hearing Sam's beautiful, slightly raspy adult voice bursting through my brain, but seeing him as a child unnerved me.

Why are you a little boy? Why aren't you a man?

"Mags, I'm Sam. It doesn't matter what I am. I'm just Sam."

I had seen hundreds of pictures of Sam when he was a little boy. Julie had always been a prolific picture taker, diligent in recording Sam's memories in carefully crafted photo albums. I would've recognized young Sam anywhere, at any angle, and with any expression. Even during their worst times, Julie had been adamant about preserving every moment she could in Sam's life so he would have something to look back to when he was older. It was her way of letting him know he was loved while making up for his father who left them when he was two.

Sam. Where are we? I realized that I didn't need to speak. He just heard me and I wasn't surprised. From the moment I met him he seemed to hear my thoughts as clearly as he knew my heart.

"We are here." Sam was matter of fact, taking my hand.

I don't understand where here is. You have to help me.

"I don't know. Maybe you're here to help me, you're here to get me out." Sam's lips were beginning to move a little, his voice still sounding very much like him as an adult, coming out of adorable five-year old him.

Get out of what?

"Get out of death, Mags. Maybe you're here to save me."

SAM STARED AT ME, WAITING, EXPECTING.

Why am I here to save you? Save you from what?

Sam smiled, his two front teeth missing like they were in his kindergarten picture, and I wanted so much to grab him and hold him tight, but I resisted.

Suddenly, we were sitting at the top of the stairs in an unfamiliar house, overlooking someone's living room. Sam sat next to me, holding me tight. We could hear yelling and crying from right below us. I looked down to see a handsome man with dark hair and brown eyes standing in front of a woman I didn't recognize, a big black duffel bag stuffed so full the zipper was almost bursting sitting on the floor next to him.

"I don't want to be with you anymore, Jules!" A man's voice was yelling loudly. "I don't love you anymore! I've found someone else who is right for me, who loves me and doesn't do stupid shit like you do. I've found someone who I'm attracted to. She isn't disgusting and fat like you are."

Jules?

I looked closely at the woman and realized it was Julie, with about thirty pounds added to her middle and everywhere else. I could feel Sam clinging to me tightly.

It's okay, I tried to whisper to him, but no sound came out.

Julie let out a sob. "Kyle, no! Please don't say things like that. I love you! Please don't go," Julie grabbed the man's arm and tried to hold on tight.

"Let go!" he said glaring at her, his eyes as hard as stone. "I haven't been able to find my love for you for a long time. I've tried, but I just can't do it anymore. You can't expect me to stay here when I'm not happy."

"No!" Julie let out a horrible scream. "What about Sam? How can you just leave Sam?"

"This is better for him!" the man said, looking away. "He wouldn't want a father like me, anyway. Do you really want him to have a father who doesn't love his mother?"

Suddenly a two-year old Sam, toddled from behind the couch.

"Da-dee," he said, reaching for the man. The man stepped back and Sam fell down, crying immediately.

"Damnit, Julie! Do you see what you did? You should've

just let me go so he wouldn't have seen me!" the man seemed visibly upset for the first time as he looked down at Sam who lay on the floor, still crying.

"Pick him up! He's your son!" Julie screeched at him as Sam wailed.

"Shut up!" the man said, his hand striking out and catching her on the cheek.

Both Julie and the man stared at one another, stunned, as her cheek began to turn red.

Sam continued to scream.

"I'll send money to you, Jules. But I don't love you anymore, and I can't live without her. I didn't mean for things to turn out this way, and I didn't mean to fall in love. It's a shitty thing to do, and I'm sorry. But the heart wants what it wants." The man got down on one knee and grabbed Sam, who fought him at first, but as the man held him tight in his own torture and pain, Sam stopped struggling and gave in. After a long moment, the man let go and stood up, giving Sam one final look as he walked out the door. He slammed the door behind him, never looking back.

Five-year-old Sam loosened his grip ever so slightly on my arm, and I realized I had been holding my breath as I'd watched the scene unfold before me. I took a deep breath and wiped my eyes.

"Do you see why I'm here?" Sam looked up at me, his eyes bigger and bluer than I had ever seen them. "If I leave here, I'll never see him again."

See who?

"My dad, Mags. It's the last time I saw him. If I leave this place, I'll never see him again because I keep getting to come back to this place and this moment, and even though it's horrible, it's the last time I got to see him, and the last time he hugged me." Sam's adult voice was cracking as his little boy face looked sadder than I could ever imagine.

But, he was mean to you! He was horrible to your mom. Why would you want to see him? Why?

"He wasn't always that way. He loved me. He did. I remember ... at least I think I remember." Five-year old Sam stood up on the step and we were eye to eye. In one sudden movement, he clasped his hand over my eyes until they were closed, and I fell into an immediate and deep sleep.

§

WHEN I OPENED MY EYES, FIVE-YEAR-OLD SAM WAS GONE, but I could hear a man singing.

I realized I was in a nursery.

Sam's father stood in the middle of the room holding a newborn baby, and I realized he was holding Sam. The man looked happy as he held Sam close, a bottle in one hand as he sang off-key.

"Sam, Sam, he's the man," Sam's father sang his own words to a tune I didn't recognize. "Sam, Sam, you're my little man."

Julie walked into the room and smiled. "How are my two men doing?"

Sam's father reached for her. "We are doing just fine. How are you doing, Mama?"

He kissed her sweetly on the cheek.

Julie smiled, looking happier than I had ever seen her, and I realized that I recognized her happiness.

It had been mine when Sam proposed to me.

§

THERE WAS A MOMENT OF DIZZINESS, AND BEFORE I realized what had happened, the scenery changed once again, and the nursery disappeared.

I was sitting on an old worn couch that didn't look familiar in Julie's living room.

The room smelled like cheap beer and was musty.

"Kid!" A voice roared through the room from up the stairs, making my heart pound. "Kid! Where are you?"

Sam came from the kitchen, cowering. He looked to be about nine-years-old, young and too skinny, so different than the five-year-old boy who had clung to me. His eyes were dark, haunted, and I could tell immediately that something wasn't right.

Sam looked at me, but didn't acknowledge me, and I wasn't sure if he could see me.

Sam. I wondered if he could hear my thoughts.

Sam ignored me.

"Come here right now, you stupid kid!" a large man appeared from the stairs that five-year-old Sam and I had been hiding on when we watched his dad leave Julie. He stood at the bottom of the stairs, course hair poking out of the top of his cotton t-shirt that was smudged with dirt. Two-day-old stubble grew out of his face, his dark eyes angry. He was big, his body thick with sagging muscle and fat, his pants sagging below his belly. "Did you get my beer?"

God, Julie. What were you thinking?

Sam held up a can of beer and gave it to the man.

"It's about time you learned who's the boss around here!" The man smacked him on the back of the head hard, and then let out a loud laugh. "When your Mama ain't home, you listen to me! She put me in charge here."

Sam's eyes flashed, and suddenly they were darker than I had ever seen them before.

Sam, no!

The man was clearly luring him in, looking for a fight, but nine-year-old Sam couldn't see it.

Sam, stop!

Sam looked directly in my eyes and I knew he saw me.

"The word is 'isn't', asshole." Sam said, his nine-year-old voice harder than I had ever heard it, even as an adult, as he squared off with the man.

The man grinned slowly.

"What did you call me?" he asked, towering over Sam, his meaty hands making a fist.

Sam, run! Get away from him!

Sam continued to ignore me.

"I said *asshole*, asshole," Sam repeated himself, louder. There was no fear in his voice as I felt myself trembling inside.

I cringed.

The man reached for Sam, grabbing a piece of his shirt, but Sam was too fast as he wriggled out of his grasp and bolted out of the house.

"Come back here, you little shit! Come back here!"

Sam turned around and stuck his middle finger up at the man as he continued to scream obscenities at Sam.

"You'll have to come home sometime!" the man yelled as Sam continued to run. I realized that I was following him, though I was never out of breath.

After a long while, Sam stopped running.

Sam! What are you doing? Why would you do that? Why would you make him so mad like that?

Sam smiled at me, his two front teeth grown in, his smile perfect. "Mags, that guy is such a douchebag. My mom dates him for a short time, and he only gets a hold of me once. He puts me in the hospital, but then he goes to jail."

I wanted to scold the nine-year-old Sam for saying "douchebag", but I realized he wasn't really a nine-year-old kid. He was my Sam.

Sam, why are we here? Why are you here? Just come back to me. Is it that difficult for you to do?

"I don't know why I'm here, Mags." I was becoming more accustomed to Sam's voice coming from the mouths of the children. "I just know that I can't leave. I don't want to leave. I don't know if I ever want to leave."

Your childhood wasn't a happy one, Sam. God, I'm so sorry that I didn't know. Why would you want to stay here?

"Because, Mags, this is what I really know. This is my life, and as messed up as it is, I know what to expect here. I don't know what to expect if I marry you, and if we have a kid. I knew the moment I met you that you were the other half of me. I've always known that I was looking for you for reasons that I just can't explain, but then I realized that I could end up being just like my mom was, or just like my dad. Things are good now, but I don't see how they are going to be good forever, and ... I just don't know if I want to come back to you."

Everything shifted, and suddenly I felt dizzy, trapped. I looked around, desperate for a way to get back to where I was before I met young Sam. I need to get out of here, right now, Sam! I need to get back. How do I get back?

"Mags, stop! Stop!" Nine-year-old Sam was tugging on my arm. "Mags, I'm sorry. That's not what I meant! I didn't mean that exactly. Please stop freaking out."

What did you mean then, Sam? I was angry with him. I had never been that angry with him before, but I was furious.

"I meant ... I'm scared. I don't know how to be an adult. I don't know how to live as an adult. The only reason I made it through college and became a somewhat normal person is because you were there to steer me in the right direction. Growing up sucked for me, and the only reason I got into college is because, at the time, the only good guy my mom ever really dated saw my potential and helped me with all of the tests and paperwork and crap before he dumped her. But my life isn't what you think it was. My mom, had lots of ...

problems. There are a lot of things you don't know about. That guy, the hairy asshole, wasn't even the worst of them ... wasn't the worst of everything that I went through. Her problems ... left their mark on me. Maybe not physically, but mentally and all of that shit." Sam pulled me down to the ground and sat on my lap, like a child would. It felt awkward and strange and normal at the same time.

I'm sorry, Sam. I had no idea. Why didn't you ever tell me about any of that?

"I wanted you to think that I was normal, and that I could be normal. I wanted you to think that I would be able to be a good dad to our kids, a good husband. But the truth is, I've been lying to you. I don't know what I'm doing. I love you, and I can't imagine living without you, but I don't know if I can do this with you ... or with anyone. When I gave you the ring, it hit me for the first time what I was doing, and I really thought I could do this, but now I don't know if I can."

I put my hand on the top of his head, like I often did when he was upset.

I began to feel the familiar dizziness again as the desperation welled up in me, and I fought it with everything I had. I didn't want to see anymore of Sam's life. I just wanted to stay here with him and figure out a way to bring him back to me.

Damn it! I didn't want to leave nine-year-old, Sam. He needed me.

## 15

## SINS OF THE MOTHER

# M aggie

I was back in Julie's living room. The smelly couch was gone, replaced by the comfortable more familiar couch I was accustomed to.

The house was eerily quiet.

Something drew me upstairs, and I walked up feeling as though I were in a trance. I looked in Sam's bedroom to find it empty. I felt as though I was floating down the hall toward Julie's room, and I heard the soft sound of crying.

A voice was speaking, but I couldn't understand it. As I got closer to Julie's room, I realized it was Julie's voice, though it sounded strange and thick. "Tell Sam I'm sorry. Tell. Sam. I'm. Sorry. Tell. Sam. Tell. Sam."

I followed the sound of her voice into her bedroom and found it empty, the only light on in her bathroom. I looked around the disheveled room, and my stomach sank as I saw a syringe and the remnants of whatever had been in the syringe, sitting on the nightstand. It looked like it had been there for quite a while, nearly crusted to the table. I dared not touch it, though something drew me to it.

I felt strangely sick, my stomach turning as I opened the door. It took a moment to process what I was seeing. The bathtub full of red, the pills strewn all over the tile floor, the half empty bottle of vodka.

I fought the urge to cry as I took in Julie's naked, gaunt body, ribs sticking out, and her cheekbones high and prominent. Her blue eyes were cloudy and half closed, her lips dry and crusted. The bathtub became redder as the blood oozed slowly from the wound in her right wrist.

"Tell Sam. Tell him." Julie looked directly into my eyes, fighting to stay conscious. "Tell him I'm sorry."

The moment froze in time as desperation flooded over me. I need to get help. I need to go ...

"Mom! Oh, God, Mom! What the hell are you doing?!" Sam's cries exploded in the doorway. He swore as he shakily dialed 911.

Julie continued to stare at me, though I wasn't sure if she was seeing me, and for a split second, I thought I was looking at my own face on hers. I furiously rubbed my eyes staring at me, wondering if I was losing my mind, my face no longer reflecting back at me, my heart pounding in my throat.

I heard Sam talking to the operator as I desperately searched for signs of the Julie I knew buried deep somewhere within.

Wake up! Julie, wake up!

Long moments went by as Sam held her hand and whispered to himself. He didn't seem to be at all fazed by her nakedness.

Sam, Sam. Can you hear me? Are you okay? Sam. I'm here. It'll be okay.

He ignored me, though I saw his back stiffen as though he heard me. He stayed focused on Julie as he placed the back of her hand on his forehead, tears flowing down his cheeks.

I stared at him, helplessly, trying to gauge how old he was. He looked to be twelve or thirteen, but his dark blue eyes told a very different story. His eyes had aged tremendously since he was nine, and I wondered what had happened between then and now.

The sound of sirens wailed in the background, getting louder as they got closer. Voices called out from the bottom of the stairs, and a flurry of activity came through like a whirl-wind as paramedics hurried in and out, taking Julie and Sam with them.

I was tethered to Sam, and I went with him in the ambu-lance as we raced through the city toward the hospital where they checked Julie in, leaving Sam outside in the waiting area.

The moments flew by in slow motion as I watched the trauma etch further into Sam's young face.

When he got word that Julie was stable, he walked out of the hospital and down the sidewalk.

Sam, where are you going?

"I'm going away from there. They'll have children's services coming after me. I have to go to my aunt's until Mom gets home." He reached in his pocket and pulled out a pack of cigarettes, tears still flowing freely from his eyes.

Sam! Don't smoke.

"Mags, I've been smoking since I was eleven." Sam said, matter-of-factly.

Oh, God. Eleven? You'll be dead by the time we're forty if you don't stop smoking. I thought you started when you were seventeen.

"That's because that's what I told you," Sam voice was hard, unfeeling. He was so different than the man I knew. I

79

barely knew who this Sam was. He was a stranger to me, and it scared me.

"It was you, Mags," Sam said, as though reading my mind while he wiped the tears away.

What was me?

"I'm a different person because of you. The moment I met you, I knew my life would never be the same. You made me want to be more than I ever imagined I could be. Because of you I wanted to be a better person. Hell, I've even cut back on my smoking because of you. It was always you." In the evening light, Sam's eyes were a deep dark blue, my favorite color. I found myself drawn to him as I moved closer, feeling myself pulled in like I always did when I was close to him.

Oh, God, you're only twelve or something like that! I jumped back, remembering this wasn't Sam, the man. He was still Sam, the boy. A child!

"I'm thirteen," Sam laughed, the tears gone. "Don't worry, I won't turn you into a felon or anything."

Thank God for that. I could never live with myself. I could see a glimpse of my Sam in the boy, and I started to feel relieved.

You should have told me about your life, Sam. It wouldn't have mattered to me. All of this pain you've held inside of you. How could you not share it with me? What happened to your mom?

"I didn't want you to think of me differently. I didn't want you to know that my mom was a train wreck, and that she went through seven different jobs between the time I was twelve and fourteen. I didn't want you to know that her boyfriends used to use me as a punching bag, and that my father never saw me after he left when I was two. Her depression was horrible for both of us, all the ups and down she put us through when she wouldn't take her medicine. It was hell, and I didn't want you to know any of it.

"You always thought I was better than I was. How would you ever look at me the same if you knew all that shit?" Sam took a long drag from his cigarette.

Sam, it wouldn't have mattered to me at all. It only would have made me love you more. My heart was shattered into a thousand pieces for the child Sam, and for Julie. I knew that only love could put it back together, his love and my love.

"How would you love me more? I'm damaged, screwed up in the head. I could become like either of my parents at any point, an abandoning cheat, or a crazy person." Sam hung his head, refusing to look at me.

Do you honestly think you're either of those things?

"I think that if you hadn't come into my life, I would've definitely been an alcoholic, which doesn't help if you're crazy. I was already there, and my track record with women before you ... well let's just say, it was questionable. You're the only woman I've ever been completely faithful to, or even wanted to be faithful to. Nothing felt right until you, as though I was waiting for you my entire life ... " Sam's voice trailed off, full of shame and regret.

You didn't answer my question, Sam. Do you really think you're like either of your parents?

"I don't know, Mags. It's too soon to tell. I know that I could be. Do you really want to find out? I don't think my dad thought he was a bad guy until suddenly he woke up one day and he was. Do you want me to leave you after we've had our first kid, like my dad left me?" Sam asked after a long pause.

Sam, you are not the sum of your past. If that were the case, I would've either become my mother, or I would've allowed her to turn me into an anorexic, pill popper. You and I are the embodiment of our *own* choices, which will be our future, and we have chosen one another. You are good, and I love you with all of my heart. My life has never been so amazing and full as it's been since you came into my life. And my life will never be the same if you don't come back to me.

"I sat in that job interview today, and it dawned on me. This isn't fair to you. I can't ask you to have a life with me when I don't think I can give you the life you deserve. Then 'BAM', that car hit me, and sometime when I was in and out of consciousness I realized that I don't want to put you through this. You don't really know me, Mags. You just think you do because I made you think I was something else, but I can't do this to you. I can't hurt you. All of a sudden, some-how, you end up here, with me, and I don't know if this is real or a dream. But now you've seen the part of me that I've hidden from you, and I just don't think I can be with you anymore."

Sam stubbed out his cigarette, picking up his pace as the evening grew later and longer.

When we arrived at his aunt's cute little Tudor, he reached under the doormat and found the key.

I love you, Sam. Please, stop saying these things. Please, I don't care about any of it. I just want to be with you. Maybe I'm here so I can love you entirely and completely. Please, don't push me away. I'm connected to you in my heart and soul and everything within me! You must know this.

"Mags, I've never let myself love anyone but you, but I am who I am, and you deserve to be loved better. You deserve so much more. Don't hate me, Mags, please." His voice had a strange sense of finality to it.

Sam ... Please ... wait ...

Sam opened the door to the house and disappeared inside, flashing me a beautifully sad smile before he shut the door.

## 16

## AWAKE

# M aggie

I WOKE UP, WITH A START, CONFUSED, MY HEAD POUNDING and fuzzy.

I sat up and looked around at the strange but familiar surroundings. I rubbed my eyes, and after a few long moments realized that I was back in Sam's hospital room. I looked down at my hands that had been holding Sam's. They were empty and so was the bed.

"THEY TOOK HIM DOWN FOR SOME MORE TESTS." JULIE looked ragged. She'd been sleeping uncomfortably in the lounge and had come to Sam's room to find me. "You wouldn't wake up, and the nurses said just to leave you in his room. They said you were exhausted. Since they've taken him down, they said we should go get some coffee or something to eat in the cafeteria."

I was in a daze as we walked, bits and pieces of my time with Sam coming back to me. Was it a dream? Had I dreamt it all? Nothing made sense. None of what I had seen had ever been told to me by Julie or by Sam. Maybe it was all just a crazy, weird dream. Maybe I just imagined it all. How is it even possible that I could go back into Sam's past and see him there as a child?

How could that ever be?

Julie was tired, but healthy. My brain was trying to catch up with the present, but was lagging desperately behind. I tried to shake my head, hoping that a large cup of coffee would help wake me up and bring me back to current reality.

"Can I ask you a question? A personal question?" I asked, hesitant, my tongue thick and my head splitting. If any of it was true, Julie had been through so much, but I had to know. "When did Sam's dad leave?"

Julie looked surprised and then sad as though the memory was too hard to confront, even twenty-one years later. "Sam was two," she said softly as we approached the cafeteria.

"I'm sorry I asked. Sam is always very vague about it, and I just wondered. I know it seems strange to ask, but I just wanted to know. " She tried unsuccessfully to keep the pain from spreading across her pretty face, attempting to hide it as she poured herself some coffee and busied herself by adding cream and sugar. She sat next to me. I looked down, and for the first time, I noticed the large bracelet she wore on her right wrist. I tried to recall a time I hadn't seen her with a bracelet on that wrist, and I couldn't.

"The day he left is just a bad memory. You'd think I would be over it by now, but ..." Her voice trailed off. "I suppose I should just learn to let go of it."

Julie attempted a smile as she grabbed a muffin. I stared at the muffins, which normally looked appetizing, but I stuck with my coffee, still not feeling myself. My stomach had been doing small flips, and I tried to ignore the nausea that refused to go away ever since I had awoken.

I couldn't take my eyes off Julie. The image of her pale skeletal body half-dead in the bathtub stayed with me, burned in my brain. Her voice echoed strangely in my ears as I tried to grasp onto the current reality of her standing next to me in the same hospital over a decade later. "Did you ever try and date again? Did you ever try and find someone?" I asked as we walked back to the family lounge, pressing her just a little farther.

"Y-y-yes. I did. But ..."

"But what?" I asked, taking her hand as we walked, not caring what anyone thought.

"But I didn't always make such great choices, and eventually after ... after ... well, eventually I just gave up. I stopped trying. I couldn't keep putting Sam through that over and over. So, it just became he and I, which worked out better anyway. I had other ... things I had to deal with. Why all of the questions?" Julie looked at me strangely, on guard. We had talked about so many things over the years, but never the past. Never <u>her</u> past, and she was suspicious.

I looked at my ring, still bright and flashing on my hand.

"I feel as though there is so much of Sam's life I am missing. And I just want to know as much as I can about him. He knows <u>everything</u> about me, and I feel as though I've ignored parts of his life that were important."

"You know all you need to know, sweetie. Sam loves you very much, and so do I ..."

Just as we made it back to the lounge the phone rang, causing us both to jump.

"Hello? Yes ... it's me. I'm Julie Connors." Julie asked, shakily. "Yes, of course."

"What's going on?" I asked as she hung up the phone.

"They want us to come to Sam's room. He's awake."

As we ran to his room, my heart was pounding. He's awake! He's awake!

We stopped, nearly running into one another as we approached his room. When we got there, the glass door was closed, and we could hear voices inside. Anxious to get in, we paced outside. I swore as I realized that in my haste, I had left my coffee in the cafeteria. But as the adrenaline coursed through me, I finally felt awake and focused for the first time in days. I was ready to face whatever was in front of us, and as long as he was awake, we had a chance. I had discovered something, even though I wasn't sure exactly what it was. I knew that it would bring us closer to one another. It had to.

It felt like hours before they opened the doors, and when they finally did, we tumbled in. There he was, his eyes a deep dark blue. He stared blankly at me as we rushed in.

I wasn't sure what I had hoped for, but to my horror, when we were finally face-to-face, I was met with nothingness, and I realized that my worst nightmare had come true.

§

THE NEXT FOUR WEEKS WERE CRITICAL AS HE REGAINED HIS strength and tried to re-learn things he had lost while in the accident.

In his reawakened state, he was a stranger to me, often shunning me from his room and asking only for Julie to stay.

"I don't need you," he said, impatiently.

I skulked around the family lounge like a stalker waiting for any sign that he wanted me to be near him. Julie repeatedly tried to send me back to our apartment to rest, but I refused. I couldn't stand the thought of not being near him in case he asked for me, though he never did. When I finally found the nerve to go to his room because I was too frustrated to wait any longer, he sat and stared straight ahead as though he was unable to stand my presence for too long.

The doctors told me to be patient. "It may just be a result of the accident, and you'll need to give him some time."

I was desperate. "I don't understand it, Julie. Why doesn't he want me to be in the room with him? What is wrong with him?"

"I don't know, Maggie. Don't forget that the doctors said to just give him some time because he's been through a lot, and he's not himself." Julie was forced in the middle against her will. The dark shadows under her eyes showed how much it wore on her.

"Please, just talk to him for me. Please!" I begged, the tears flowing freely as they had for days and weeks.

I spent days sinking into the couches of the family lounge as I thought about my dream and willed myself to remember those moments with Sam as a young boy. Hazy moments floated back to me, and I began to understand that there had been truth to his words, even though I didn't realize it then. I began to wonder if it had been a dream after all, and if it hadn't, what had it been? A connection? A glitch in time? How was it even possible that I could've been there? It didn't make any sense.

After one month of Sam being awake, he finally asked for me to come to the room to see him. I had been desperately waiting for him to want me, and I ran to his room, my heart skipping with anticipation.

As I walked into his room I was filled with hope, but when I saw the look on his face, my heart stopped completely, a sharp pain immediately crushing the excitement I had felt.

He looked like a stranger as he gazed at me with dark, expressionless eyes, and suddenly I felt as though I was going to die.

## 17

# THE END

M aggie

I STOOD TWO STEPS INTO THE DOORWAY, FROZEN.

"I'm sorry, Mags," was all he said. The voice that I loved so much, that had once sent shivers through me, was strange and distant.

"I'm sorry, Mags," Sam repeated.

I stared at him, uncertain of what he meant, unsure of what to say. He turned his head and looked toward the window, refusing to make eye contact with me.

"'I'm sorry, Mags?' What are you saying, Sam? What do you mean?" I moved toward him trying to understand his words.

"You know me. You know what I am saying to you," Sam said, still looking outside as though there was something more interesting going on out there than the explosion that was happening two feet from him.

"No! I don't," I said challenging him. "Explain this to me."

He was silent, his expression completely empty.

"Why are you doing this?" I asked, my voice rising in a near shriek. My heart felt like a heavy rock in my chest, and I could barely breathe as I gasped for air.

"I don't know, Mags. I'm sorry ... I don't know why, but something has changed. No matter what I do, I just can't make myself want to be with you again. I've tried to find it, but I just don't love you anymore. You being here in the hospital is distracting ... annoying ... and I don't want you around. I'm sorry." I barely recognized him, his voice flat but unapologetic.

Julie stood next to his hospital bed, silent, tears falling down her cheeks.

"How ..." I gasped, unable to speak. "H-h-how can you say you don't love me? How can you be so cruel? After everything that's happened between us ... all we've said to each other. How can you just throw me away ... throw *us* away? How can you do this?"

"I wish it was different. I've been waiting to feel something again, but I just don't. I can't force myself to love you. Believe me, I've tried. You being here makes me nervous and uncomfortable, and I feel bad having you around and knowing you are waiting for something that may never happen. I don't know what has changed, but I want you to go."

"Sam, how can you not remember your love for me? What about our life and everything we've done together, everything we've built?" I cried, knowing I sounded desperate but not caring. My hands were shaking, and I felt numb, my face fiery hot.

He shrugged his shoulders in silence.

"No! No!" I shook my head at him, stubbornly. "I'm not

leaving. I'm your fiancée. We are supposed to get married. I'm not just leaving."

"Mags ... I don't want to be with you anymore. I don't want to marry you. I don't know if I ever did. " Sam's voice was hard.

Before I could stop it, a painful moan escaped my lips as I felt the rock in my chest begin to crack.

"I don't want to marry you," Sam repeated, to make sure I heard it.

I opened my mouth but nothing came out, and everything seemed to move in slow motion.

"Sweetie," Julie stepped forward. "It would be better for everyone if you just left now and went home. Sam needs his space."

"Home?" I cried, looking over at Sam who stared straight ahead as though I wasn't in the room. "Home is where I live with Sam. Home is *our* apartment. You want me to go home to *our* apartment and then what do you want me to do there? Do you want me to pack up and move from there also? What do you want me to do, Sam?"

I could feel the mascara running down my face as my eyes burned. My eyelids were already beginning to get puffy, and I knew that I must look like a mess. Even all the more reason for Sam to reject me.

The crushing feeling in my chest intensified, and I wondered if I was having a heart attack.

At least I'm in the right place for it, I thought ironically.

I took a step toward Sam, willing him to look at me. I knew that the connection between us couldn't be completely gone, and within moments he was looking at me. The emptiness of his expression made me cry even harder. I didn't know how much more I could take as I silently pleaded with him.

"Please, Sam ... please ..." I cried. "What do you want me to do?"

"Maggie ..." His words erased any love that had ever been between us, sending a shudder down my spine. "I don't really care what you do."

As I ran out of the room, I could hear the faint sound of an alarm from one of the machines going off, but I couldn't stop. My world as I had known it was ending, and nothing mattered more than getting as far away from Sam as fast as I could.

## SAM

I LISTENED TO THE HARDNESS IN MY VOICE AS I TOLD HER that I didn't care about her, and I felt my soul being destroyed with my words. As I watched her walk away, tears rolling down her cheeks, barely able to speak, I've never hated myself more. I've never been more disgusted with who I am until this very moment.

She didn't deserve to be hurt this way, and I should've never gotten so close. The ring was a mistake. A big fucking mistake. What was I thinking to imagine a lifetime with a woman like her? How could I ever think I deserved her love?

I watched the doorway, wishing she'd come back. My mom left shortly after Mags did, not even bothering to look at me when she walked out. In the end, it was my decision, but she loved her as much as I did. Mags was the daughter she never had, and she wanted us to be together. She'd never understand why I had to let her go and neither do I, but something inside won't let me be happy.

I had to send her away before she found out ... what I was ... what I am. I would only end up destroying her life if she stayed with me. I knew this.

The doctor even told me that I needed to figure things out. Even he knew that I was ruining my life, and I couldn't take her along for such a horrible and bumpy ride. She deserved more. Much more.

If I had been a better man, I would've left her alone when I first saw her. I would've never asked her for tutoring. I would've spared her from ever meeting me, which means I never would've kissed her soft and perfect lips. I never would've traced her satiny skin with my fingertips, or let my mouth wander over all of her most sensitive places. I'd have never known what it was like to be with someone as perfectly delicate and beautiful as she is.

But I'm a selfish bastard, and I knew when I saw her that I had no other choice. Her eyes drew me in, her body beckoned me, and there was no way in hell that I was ever going to stay away from her.

Once I saw her it was over. I was hers, and she was mine, and now it was all over and I was never going to know the joy of her body and soul ever again.

I hated myself and all I had become, and I knew that she would end up hating me too.

## ❧ 18 ❧
## NUMB

M aggie

SOMETHING ABOUT THE WORLD DIDN'T SEEM RIGHT. FOR weeks I lay in our apartment, in *our* bed, waiting for him to come back to me.

I smelled our sheets, dreading the moment that his scent would disappear, and I prayed for him to walk back through the door and tell me that it had all been a bad dream. I waited and slept, slept and waited, barely eating or moving.

I didn't answer my phone or texts. My mother called as many as ten times a day, leaving messages until my voicemail was full. They all said the same thing.

"Maggie call me. I'm worried about you. Please."

I felt as though I was an open wound, any sound or movement sending intense pain through my entire body. I couldn't remember a day without Sam. I was convinced that I had never even been alive before I had met him. Had I? Had I lived?

Now I was alone, and he had rejected me completely.

The world was strange, and after wearing the same clothes, laying in our bed with my head on Sam's pillow, empty in every way, I realized that I needed to do something else. I could no longer wait for him to return.

Julie refused my calls, sending me straight to voicemail. Nausea came over me in waves as I was compelled to finally eat. I had begged her to pick up the phone until her phone no longer rang, and I knew that I had been blocked.

Life must go on, a tiny voice whispered in my ear. *You* must go on.

Without Sam, I couldn't bear to hear any sound and had been living in silence, afraid that even the smallest tinkle might actually shatter me completely. I slowly began to welcome noise and sound back into my life.

It had an awkward start and stop, like an old-time record player when it played vinyl records and the needle would abruptly skip. The world sounded strange; garbled and unclear.

I knew that I must call the only person who had been there my entire life. Though our relationship was often strained and awkward, I knew that my mother would come through for me, and she didn't disappoint. Within a day, she had arrived with movers and my father in-tow.

I tried to be grateful and ignore the fact that the world no longer sounded quite like it should. As I slowly packed up my things I watched as the pieces of my life were beginning to fall away and disappear, wrapped up in boxes that may never be opened again.

Pictures and love notes, all wrapped up in tissue paper and newspaper, neatly labelled and carefully preserved.

Mags and Sam, Sam and Mags.

All seemed completely lost and gone forever.

My mother was uncharacteristically kind, though still distant and strange, her pretty face forcing a smile even though I could tell that it pained her. She had been beautiful her entire life, her large brown eyes and shiny blonde hair, often making her intimidating.

"You'll get through this Maggie," she reassured me, trying to soften her voice as much as she could, my father squeezing her shoulder, encouraging her.

I was numb and empty.

I packed.

I tried to call Julie again, but my call went straight to voicemail. I threw my phone in frustration.

"Why? Why don't they talk to me? I just don't understand!" I cried out for answers as my parents looked at me blankly. They were always uncomfortable with such displays of emotion, both reserved, keeping their feeling pushed deep down in their impeccable clothing and perfect appearances.

"Maggie, please," my mother looked at me, her eyes demanding that I lower my voice.

"I can't, Mother. I need Sam," I cried out, the pain fresh as I said his name.

"Why do you need him? He doesn't want you, Maggie. He doesn't want to be with you anymore."

I gasped as though she had slapped me.

Hearing her say the words was too much, and I fought off another wave of nausea.

"I'm sorry ..." she said, sounding truly apologetic. "I didn't mean to hurt you."

"I know, but you don't understand."

"Understand what?"

I paused. I wasn't sure that I was ready to tell her. I wasn't even sure that I wanted to believe it myself.

"Understand what?" she prompted.

"I need him ... because, I'm pregnant."

Suddenly the air dissolved from the room, and before I could stop it, the world fell away, and I felt myself escape into blessed darkness.

## 19

# BANISHED

# M aggie

THE MORNING LIGHT SHONE BRIGHT INTO THE KITCHEN AS
I folded laundry in the little laundry room and kept a close
eye on the little person that poked around the kitchen cabi-
nets in search of a snack.

"Mommy," she looked up at me, her beautiful blue eyes
and dark, brown, curly hair reminded me so much of Sam.
"Hungry."

She pointed at the bananas with her chubby little fingers,
and I obliged, peeling one carefully and breaking off pieces
for her so she wouldn't choke.

"That's too big of a piece," my mother said as she walked
into the kitchen, never refraining from giving unwanted
advice. "She'll choke."

I bit my tongue, reminding myself that she was helping
me out by letting me do our laundry at her house since our

washer was broken. The next pieces I broke off were substantially smaller.

"Mmmmm," Moira said, smiling up at me. I couldn't help but scoop her up and kiss her on her soft little banana-filled cheeks.

"Mommy loves you, Moo," I said, nuzzling her neck, enjoying the soft smell of baby powder and sweetness.

"I looove you, tooo!" she said emphasizing each word by tapping my nose gently as she said each one. She giggled, making me giggle with her as she usually did.

"Mommy needs to finish laundry. Go and play and we'll be done soon." I smiled as I set her down and patted her gently on the butt, sending her on her way.

"You pick her up too much," my mother said wrinkling her nose at me. "She's going to be spoiled."

"Maybe I don't pick her up <u>enough</u>," I said, trying not to raise my voice.

"Hmfph," my mother said in disapproval, as she walked away.

"Why do you do that?" I asked, trying to keep my voice even.

My mother busied herself with the Keurig, making herself a Cappuccino. "Do what?"

"You know what. Criticize. Why do you always criticize?"

"I don't know. Maybe I criticize because I think you should do things differently. I don't mean anything by it. I just ... don't want Moira to be spoiled."

I folded laundry absently as I thought about Moira, my little Moo. She had been my saving grace, and I knew I would always pick her up as much as I wanted to. She had taken my heart and put it back together when I didn't think anyone ever could, so I would be damned if anyone ever dictated how much I picked her up!

I thought about how I hadn't known if I could have her

alone. The days during my pregnancy were the darkest of my life, and I had wondered if I would be able to see it through without Sam. He had been my rock, and living without him had seemed impossible. I had never imagined having a baby on my own and always thought he would be with me.

I didn't understand what I had done, or why I had been allowed to see into his life and his past if I wasn't going to be allowed to be a part of his future. Life seemed cold and cruel, and even though I knew the pain couldn't be good for Moira or me, I couldn't push it completely away. I held onto it, finding solace in the torture and the pain.

Strangely, the person I least expected to come to my rescue arrived when I needed her the most.

## 20

# NEW BEGINNING

# M aggie

A COUPLE OF YEARS AND AN ANGELIC TWO-YEAR-OLD HAD helped heal the most broken part of me, though I knew I still wasn't whole and might never be.

At least I no longer fell to the floor when I thought about the last time I saw him.

I no longer felt my heart shatter into a thousand sharp pieces when I pictured his face after he had gotten home a month after he had awakened from his coma. I had already packed everything up and sent it to my parents, but I'd lingered behind waiting ... and hoping. Then he had walked through the door and for a single moment I thought he might ask me to stay, but he didn't.

I had been pregnant during the time of his accident, but I hadn't told him about Moira yet, foolishly wanting to wait until he was whole to tell him about it. I thought it would bring us even closer.

Then he came home only to tell me that he was glad that I had finally accepted that it was over, and that he was leaving, too. My entire world was finally and completely destroyed.

"I'm sorry," he'd said, his voice flat and distant. "I don't know why, Mags. I don't know what happened, but I just don't love you anymore."

"I don't understand, Sam. What did I do? What could have changed while you were in the hospital? I just don't understand this!" I had been at a loss. I knew the distance between us grew even deeper with each night apart, but I thought it might change once he came home.

"It's not about you, Mags. You didn't do anything wrong. I just can't find my love for you anymore. Something has changed, but I don't know what happened." He was different, hardened, familiar yet a stranger at the same time.

"But, why don't you just give us a chance? You just got home. Once we settle in, it will be okay. I know it will." The world was moving in slow motion, and I realized that Julie's car was still waiting outside, the engine running.

The getaway car.

"You're leaving now?" I sat on the couch, suddenly feeling very heavy.

"Yes. Mags, I wasn't planning to stay. What we had was great, but this just isn't for me. I don't know what to tell you. I'm sorry." Sam was turning toward the door as I stood up quickly and grabbed him, forcing him to look at me.

"Look at me, dammit," I said, sobbing. He was no longer the Sam I loved. This Sam was someone I had never seen before, his eyes completely devoid of any warmth or love. This was the Sam I had been looking at for the past month in the hospital, but somehow I thought that being home would make him different.

"I'm sorry, Mags. But I just can't be with you anymore. You can just keep the ring. I don't have any use for it anymore. I really am sorry. I know how much you've done for me."

He turned and walked toward the door, and I realized that he'd planned to leave me when he got home all along.

I had fallen on the floor at the door when he walked out and didn't get up for two days. When I finally did wake up, the world had turned to a dull shade of grey and stayed that way for weeks.

Then Moira changed everything.

There was no longer time to lay on the floor grieving a love that wouldn't release its grip on me, no matter how much I begged it to, night after night. I surrendered and finally went to my parent's house, the one safe place that still remained. When Moira was born she became my love and my life. I was grateful for her and the unconditional love she bestowed upon me.

It was because of her I was alive and able to get up, thankful for the day.

I regretted not telling Sam about Moira when I had the chance. I wanted desperately for Sam to be a part of Moira's life and tried to tell him about Moira, but he made it clear he no longer wanted to be a part of me. My letters came back unopened, my emails and texts went unanswered, and I was blocked from him in every way. I even tried to go to Julie's apartment, but she no longer lived there, and there was no sign of her or Sam left anywhere.

After a year I stopped trying. He had clearly not found his love for me, and had made sure that I couldn't find him. He gave no choice but to live with my memories and try to purge him from my soul. But every day, Moira reminded me of him, and the struggle to forget him was tortuous and real, her tiny smile reminding me of the love that had been taken from me without explanation.

My mother had strangely tried her best to be supportive, which was unlike her, but I was thankful that she was there for me and that she offered to watch Moira anytime I needed it. I began to see a very different side of her that I wished I had seen when I was a girl.

I sighed heavily and finished folding the clothes. I gathered Moo up to return home, hoping one day I would stop wishing that Sam would finally decide that he loved me.

"Wake up Mags, you're dreaming!"

The dream had been vivid. Sam was crying and calling out for me. We were standing in a bathroom, and there was blood all over the floor. I was trying to comfort him, and he was thankful that I was there.

"I can't believe you're here, Mags," he said, smiling at me and making my heart flutter. I marveled at the whiteness of his teeth as I always had. "I'm so happy to see you."

He gathered me in his arms, and I felt myself melt against him, feeling at home immediately. As he held me close and tight, I ran my fingers down the strength of his back, my hands knowing instinctively where he liked to be touched.

"I've missed you so much," I purred into his chest.

"I've missed you too, Mags," he said, his breath hot on the top of my head, his breath quickening.

His body moved ever so slightly against mine, his hips tight against me. He was as excited as I was to be so close, and he pulled my shirt over my head with barely any effort.

"I don't know why I ever left you," he murmured against my ear as he slowly and softly kissed me from the base of my neck to the tip of my ear, leaving me gasping for air. "I'm so sorry for leaving you. I've always loved you."

"I've always loved you, too," I was crying, and I couldn't stop. "Why? Why did you stop loving me? Please ... tell me ... please!"

I was sobbing uncontrollably.

"Maggie! Maggie!"

Someone was shaking me, hard.

"Maggie! You're dreaming! Wake up, honey."

I sat straight up, trembling and sweating from my dream. It had been a long time since I had such a vivid dream about Sam. There had been a time when they came to me nightly, but they no longer haunted me like they once did.

"Are you okay?" Soft brown eyes stared at me from the other side of the bed, full of love and concern. "Are you okay, honey?"

"Yes," I said, taking deep breaths. "I'm okay."

I was upset with myself for having a dream about Sam on a day like this one.

My wedding day.

As much as I tried to let Sam go, he was always with me, and I hated myself for it. I had even allowed myself to love again. Somewhere deep down I knew I should tell my Dylan about Sam, but something inside of me couldn't.

"Don't worry, Dyl, I'll be okay. I'm ready for today." I smiled up at him as he kissed me softly on the forehead. But I wasn't sure if I was trying to convince him, or me.

## ❧ 21 ❧
## SURPRISES

# M aggie

MOIRA WAS BEAUTIFUL IN HER FLOWER GIRL DRESS, HER
soft brown ringlets falling around her shoulders, creating a
halo around her perfect head.

At five, she had her own sense of style and pale pink was
the color she chose, which proved to be a wonderful color on
her. She was the perfect combination of Sam and I, and I
thought for the thousandth time how happy and impressed
with her he would be. Julie would be smitten with her smart,
sweet granddaughter whose laugh could make the entire
world light up. But now they would never see her this way.
Ever.

"Mommy, you look beautiful," Moira said, her eyes big and
full of wonder as she stared up at me.

"Thank you, Moo." I smiled, my love for her bursting

from me as it often did. She saved me, and I never wanted to let myself forget it.

I stared at myself in the mirror. My dress was elegant, simple. Less frivolous than it would have been if I would've married Sam. I had planned years before that my dress with Sam would have been big and fluffy, and everything about our wedding would have been about celebrating our love to the heavens.

But with Dylan, it was different.

He was a great guy, a doctor, and while our love wasn't the passionate ride it had been with Sam, it was solid and good and exactly what I needed to ground me. I had finally accepted that I couldn't keep Sam in my heart my entire life, even though Moira was a constant reminder of everything I had lost.

"Are you ready?" my dad wiped his brow nervously as he looked down at me and smiled.

"Yes, Dad, I'm ready," I said, confidently.

The music cued up, and I could hear the traditional wedding march as I held tightly to Dad's arm.

I floated down the aisle feeling all eyes turn to stare at me. I heard collective "oohs" and "ahhs" as we made it down without incident. I looked up to see Dylan, his big brown eyes tearing up behind his wire rimmed glasses. He was handsome in his traditional black tux, every bit the 'hot doctor' he was known as at the hospital. I had met him through a friend when I was least expecting it and fell for him as much as my stunted heart would allow. He was good to me, and I did love him.

We had been dating for a little over two years when he finally convinced me that we were good together and should get married, and much to my surprise, I agreed.

Moira called him 'Daddy Dylan', though she had nobody

else to compare him to except for her Papa. She had made it through most of her young life without a father figure, but with Dylan, she felt safe, and he was a natural with kids. She was happy that 'Daddy Dylan' would be there to stay and that we would all get to live in a house and get to leave the 'part-ment.' I hadn't given up the apartment yet, but knew I would have to say good-bye to the place where I'd finally found myself once again.

I had finally given up on the fantasy I would come home to find Sam waiting for me. I was ready to move on, and Dylan was everything I hoped I would find one day, and more.

"Do you, Margaret Elizabeth take Dylan Edward ..." the pastor continued, but I was lost in my memories.

"I do," I said automatically.

Dylan looked at me, one eyebrow raised like he did when he knew I wasn't completely there. I could feel my cheeks get hot, and I turned to the pastor and tried to concentrate. Dylan smiled at me and nodded, almost as if to say calm down, like he often did.

"I do," he said, responding appropriately, unlike me who had answered the question before it was completely asked.

"... I now pronounce you husband and wife ..."

The ceremony was already over, and I turned suddenly, catching my heel on my dress.

"I have you! You're okay." Sam's voice whispered in my ear.

I looked up as Sam's eyes, aqua, were staring into mine.

"Sam, where have you been?" I cried.

There was a collective gasp from the audience.

"Are you okay, honey? Did you just call me Sam?" Dylan asked, standing me up with ease as he allowed me to lean against him for support.

"I need some air," I said, feeling faint again.

"Mommy," Moira said, grabbing my hand and shaking it.

"Yes, Moo?" I asked, trying to take deep breaths.

"Mommy, look." Moira pointed to the lone figure sitting in the last pew in back of the church. I took a sharp breath in, right before the room turned black.

Aqua blue eyes and chestnut hair.

Sam!

I WOKE UP, MY HEAD POUNDING, AND COULD HEAR HUSHED voices outside of the room.

"I'm sorry. I don't know what I was thinking. I shouldn't have come. I'm sorry." I could hear Sam's deep voice apologizing, repeatedly.

"Why are you here?" Dylan's voice sounded strained, even through the door.

"I'm sorry ... I'm sure you know that I'm Mags' ex-fiancé. I don't know what I was thinking. I just ... I don't know why I came." Sam's voice lowered, and I couldn't hear what he was saying.

Suddenly, my mother came into the room, her face set in an expression I didn't recognize. My throat was dry, and the glass of water in her hand appeared like an oasis before me.

I gulped the water down, not caring that it dribbled down my face and onto my dress. My hair was surely a mess by now with my makeup, no doubt, running down my face.

"Well, this is a train wreck," Mother said, her voice strange. She looked oddly composed for a woman whose daughter had passed out at her own wedding at the sight of her ex-fiancé in front of a church full of people after saying his name.

"Yes," I croaked out. "I'm sorry, Mother. I know how much you and Daddy paid for ..."

"It's funny that Sam waited until today to decide to make his appearance," Mother said interrupting me.

"Yes," I said, confused about the direction she was taking. I had expected anger, rage, or frustration. But this almost felt ... comforting.

"Technically, you're married, you know," Mother said, sitting next to the couch where I was laying.

"I know," I said, unable to say anything else.

"What do you want to do, Margaret Elizabeth?"

Her question caught me off guard, and I looked at her, stunned. Her face was a mask of composure, and I found it impossible to read what she was thinking.

"What do you mean?" I asked, not sure if I heard her correctly.

"It's not a difficult question, Maggie. What do you want to do? Do you want to stay married to Dylan, or do you want to try and ride off into the sunset with Sam?" Mother was staring at my head, puzzled as she tried to put my disheveled hair back together.

"I don't even know why Sam is here. I mean ... why would he come here now?" I said, wondering where my mother was, and who this woman was in front of me.

"I suppose you should probably find out, then," Mother said, smiling. When she smiled, her face was pretty, and I thought we looked alike. But this smile was different than anything I had ever seen coming from her before. This one was true and real, and I felt the warmth of it fill me from the inside out. "Maggie, I know you think I don't like you, which is the farthest thing from the truth. Both of my parents lacked any show of emotion, so it's hard for me and always has been. When I married your father, somehow I thought it would be easier to show love, but it wasn't. Instead, I became exactly like my parents, and I'm sorry about that because it made me a terrible mother. But somehow, Moira has changed that for me."

I was stunned and silent.

All my life she had been distant, almost cruel, but this was the woman I had always longed for, and I felt myself give into her. Other than Sam, there was nothing else I had ever wanted more in my entire life than her.

THE KNOCK ON THE DOOR INTERRUPTED OUR MOMENT, AND my mother stood up to answer it as though she knew who was on the other side. The voices had disappeared from outside of the room, and I wondered if Sam had left, ignoring the part of me that desperately wished he would still be here.

I braced myself, unsure of who would be there, not ready to face Dylan, but not ready to face Sam, either.

"Diane," Sam's voice flooded through me, warming me as I felt the blood rushing through my body.

"Sam. What great timing you have," my mother said, her voice flat, her brown eyes hard though a polite smile played on her perfect face.

"Yes ma'am," Sam mumbled, entering the room, careful not to get too close to her.

"I'll be outside if you need me, Margaret," Mother said, looking directly at Sam.

I stood up, trying to smooth my hair, my heart pounding so loud I was sure he would hear it.

"Hey," Sam said, slowly meeting my gaze.

"Hi," I said, looking at him and not saying another word. He looked exactly the same only the lines around his eyes were a little deeper and his hair slightly longer than I had ever seen it before. I reminded myself to breathe as his blue eyes stared directly into mine, and I realized that he still had the same effect on me. I cursed myself with every word I knew for being so weak and falling so quickly under his spell.

He was staring at me in my wedding dress, his eyes filling with tears.

"God Mags, I-I-I'm sorry. I don't know what the hell I was thinking. I just got back in town and saw that you were getting married in the newspaper. I told myself I wasn't going to come, but I went for a walk, and somehow I ended up here. I just couldn't help it. I'm so sorry." Sam wiped the tears away with the back of his hand, and I wanted desperately to put my hand on his head and comfort him like I used to. "I just had to see you ... and the girl. I hate to assume, but she's mine, right? I mean ... God, she looks just like me."

I couldn't speak. A thick lump had formed in the middle of my dry throat and I was crying, unable to help myself as the tears ran shamefully down my cheeks.

I nodded, thankful that he recognized himself in her, relief and sadness flooding over me all at once.

He smiled, a small thoughtful smile, as he ran his fingers through his thick, dark hair, an old habit I remember seeing when he was nervous or upset.

"Sam, I have to ask you this. Why?" I managed to croak out, my voice barely a whisper. "W-w-why did you leave me?"

Sam took a step toward me, and I jumped back as though he were a snake about to wrap himself around my neck. I didn't know what would happen if he touched me, and I wasn't ready to take any chances. I reminded myself that despite everything, I was married. I had said 'I do', even though I wasn't sure Dylan would want to stay married now.

"I didn't really leave you, Mags. You left me," Sam said,

shaking his head. "When I got home, you were already packed up. I just ... finished it for us."

"What? No! I didn't leave you. You shut me out and left me in complete silence! Don't you dare make it my fault!" I said, immediately frustrated. How could he say that I left him after all I had been through?

"I'm sorry ... I know. It was my fault. I convinced myself that I was wrong to love you. There was a lot going on, a lot that I couldn't tell you and still can't tell you. It's the oldest excuse in the book, I know. I'll tell you one day, but I can't tell you right this moment."

"But how could you just refuse to see me and cut me out of your life so completely? I just don't understand it." All the pain flooded through me, and I felt as though I was being thrust back six years ago.

"There were things that happened to me when I was young, things you wouldn't have understood. My mom was a mess after my dad left. She ... tried to kill herself, and I knew that it must be my fault. I knew that I should've made her want to live more ... I wanted you to know, I wanted to tell you and for you to see it, but I couldn't. I knew you would see me differently ..." Sam said, his head in his hands.

I grabbed him suddenly, my stomach dropped, and my chest felt as though it was going to explode. His flesh felt like it was burning against my fingers, but I held onto him, desperate for him to understand. " I did see it, Sam! When you were in the coma, and I was at the hospital, I did see it. You made me see it, and I saw the moment when your father left, and then the big, ugly man who tried to beat you because you called him an asshole ... I saw all of it!"

Sam stared at me, stunned, his eyes wider than I had ever seen.

"I didn't ... what are you saying, Mags?"

"I saw everything. It was like I was there."

Neither of us dared breathe, the air around us completely still.

"So ... it was real," he said, his voice low and thick with emotion.

"What was real?" I asked, still holding onto his wrists.

"Y-y-you were there. I did talk to you when I was a kid, you were with me. I remember. I remember all of it. I thought it was a dream this entire time. I thought I just made it up when I was in the coma. H-h-how could you have been with me when I was a kid? How could you have seen those things? How?"

I let go of Sam's wrists, not sure if I was hearing him correctly.

"You remember seeing me?" I thought they had been dreams, induced by many sleepless nights in the hospital and a desire for him to wake up. I had convinced myself they weren't real and that I had been dreaming the entire time, miraculously seeing into his past. I hadn't imagined that the conversations were real, or that he could've really seen me. "You remember me being there with you?"

"Yes. You were always so familiar from the first moment I met you, but it never made sense until now. It doesn't seem possible, but you were there with me." Sam stepped closer, and before I could stop him, he was holding me in his arms. My knees let go, and he sank to the floor with me, holding me close, whispering my name over and over in my ear.

I leaned against him, feeling the warmth of his breath on my head, his arms tightening around me. Time stood still, and I felt myself never wanting to leave those moments ever again. Being in his arms was like being home. I had missed him so much, the emptiness without him catching up with me.

As I caught a glimpse of the light from my rings, I

couldn't ignore that something in my heart just didn't feel right.

"Maggie!" Dylan said, suddenly standing over us, his fists clenched as tears ran down his face. He had walked in silently, neither of us realizing it. He stared at us as though he had walked in to see us naked, and I immediately felt guilty.

Sam held tight to me, unwilling to let go as I suddenly realized that I was trapped in my worst nightmare.

## 22

# CHOICES

# M aggie

I JUMPED UP QUICKLY AND HEARD A RIPPING SOUND. I KNEW immediately that I had ripped the back of my dress but didn't care as I stood in front of Dylan, disheveled and still a mess.

I could still feel Sam's fingers on my skin as though they remained there, burning into me. He had reluctantly let me go when I stood up, but lingered close as Dylan kept his eyes on him, a hard expression on his face.

"I'm sorry, Dylan. I'm so sorry I ruined everything. It was supposed to be a wonderful, perfect day and ..." My heart ached as I watched his fists unclench, and he wiped the tears from under his wire rimmed glasses.

"What are we doing Maggie? Are we going to end this just as it's beginning? Are you going back to this guy after what he did to you?" Dylan pointed at Sam angrily.

"H-h-how do you know what happened?" I had been careful not to talk about Sam to Dylan other than to tell him he was Moira's father. I hadn't wanted him to hear anything in my voice that would reveal the love I had hidden away for Sam. I knew I had betrayed Dylan by keeping it from him, but I had convinced myself that it would disappear once it was replaced by Dylan's love.

"He told me everything," Dylan said. "I didn't want to believe that you loved each other so much, but now that I am looking at you, I can see it in your face. I knew you were holding something back from me Maggie, but I thought when you said that you would marry me, that things would be different. I guess I was wrong."

"No ... Dylan, no," I shook my head in confusion as Dylan stepped closer to me and grabbed my hands, holding them tight.

"I love you and Moira, very much, Maggie. I don't want to live without you, but seeing you and ... him, and the way you looked at him ..." his eyes moved between me and Sam, flickering between pain and anger. I wanted to say so much, but my mouth was dry and the words refused to come. "I love you ... but I just can't live with you knowing that you love someone else so much. I've done this before, and I can't do it again. That's just not for me."

Dylan kissed my hand and I watched him as he pulled my rings off my finger, his dark eyes never leaving mine. He took his ring off and put them all in his breast pocket.

"I'll have the marriage annulled the first chance I get. I'll go say good-bye to Moira." I wanted to grab and hold onto him and beg him not to give up on me yet, but I knew from the look in his eyes that he wouldn't welcome my touch. I was at a loss for words as he gave Sam one last hard look before he turned and walked out the door.

I turned to Sam, my heart aching for Dylan, feeling as though a piece had been ripped out from inside of me.

"I'm sorry this happened," Sam said, taking my hand, trying to comfort me.

"You're sorry?" I turned and yelled at him, angrily. "Why would you come back now, today of all days? Why didn't you come back years ago? Why wouldn't you just answer my calls when I called to tell you about Moira? Why NOW!?"

Sam looked like he wanted to answer, but nothing came out of his mouth. I fixed my eyes on his lips, the ones I had kissed a thousand times; the same ones that were burned onto mine so that nobody's kiss would ever stir so much inside of me ever again.

As I stared at them now, I realized that they just looked like anyone else's lips, the magic gone as they remained still with so many words left unspoken.

"I can't ... do this with you right now, Sam. I hurt Dylan, and I love him. I just can't let him think that he doesn't matter to me. I want you to meet Moira, but I just can't do this right now." I grabbed a piece of paper from the desk in the room and scribbled on it. "Here is my number. You can call me."

Sam took a step toward me, and I was inexplicably pulled in as I had been so many years before. There was a connection between us that was as strong and palpable as it had ever been, drawing us in, insisting that we touch.

As I stepped away from him without allowing him to touch me, my feet moving in slow motion, I felt the bond weaken as Sam's face fell, reflecting the turmoil I felt within my own soul. I closed my eyes and willed myself to step away. As I walked out the door, the connection between us broke. I strangely felt free.

"MOMMY, WHERE ARE WE GOING? WHERE DID DADDY Dylan go?" Moira sat in the back seat of my car, kicking the back of my seat.

"Moo, stop kicking, honey. We're going to find Daddy Dylan now." I pulled out of the church parking lot carefully. There had still been plenty of wedding guests milling about, many of them gave me dirty looks as I pulled Moira past them. I wished I had bothered to fix my hair again after mother fixed it. It had permanently and catastrophically fallen out of the updo it was secured in at the beginning of this horrendous day. My face was even worse with long lines of black eyeliner streaking under each eye from the tears, lipstick smudged on my face. I looked like a hooker, and I felt horrible for Moira who had to be seen with me.

I glanced down at my phone to see if Dylan had called, but there were no missed calls.

I cursed under my breath and glanced in the rearview mirror at Moira, who sat still as she stared out of the window singing quietly to herself. I fought the urge to speed through the city with Moira in the back seat, praying he would be home.

After what felt like a lifetime, we pulled up in front of Dylan's house, which was supposed to be my house, too.

"Mommy," Moira's sweet voice came from the back seat.

"Yes?"

"Why were you crying? Who was that man at the church who made you cry?"

"Moira, not right now. I need to see Daddy Dylan."

"But who was he? Do I know him? I didn't rec'nize him," Moira curiosity had been awakened, and I knew there would be no silencing her until I answered her questions.

"Come, Moo," I said pulling her out of the car and walking her to the front steps of the house where I sat down next to her.

"But Mommy ... who was it?" Moira could be relentless when she wanted to know something, and I knew that I had no choice but to tell her.

"That man was ... Sam ... your daddy."

Moira looked at me with confusion in her blue eyes, so much like Sam's.

"Daddy Dylan?"

"No, Moo. Your real daddy." We had talked about her 'real' daddy many times since she started school and began wondering why a lot of the other kids had daddies but she didn't.

"Oh." Moira was quiet, playing with her fingers. "Where did he come from?"

"I don't know, Moo. I don't know where he came from, or why he decided to come back to us after all of this time." As frustrated as I was with Sam, I tried to hide it. I envisioned the three of us together, laughing, lying on a hammock or taking a walk, but as quickly as the thoughts entered my mind, I shook them out. How could I ever trust him now after everything we'd been through, and how he left? How could I do this to Dylan who had helped bring me back to life?

"Do you want him to be my daddy instead of Daddy Dylan?" Moira took my face between her hands, her little nose pointed right on mine so that her big eyes were close and blurry. "Well, do you? Answer me!"

I pulled my head back, careful to let her keep her soft hands on my cheeks. She was so different than me, so bossy and opinionated. Unlike me, she wasn't afraid of anything. "I don't know what I want to do, Moo. I don't know."

"You're a grown up. You should know things," she said looking at me, disappointed. She pulled herself on my lap and leaned against me, knowing somehow that I needed to be comforted.

"Maggie? Moira?" Dylan's warm voice, full of reservation and surprise, echoed behind me.

I stood up awkwardly in my dress, grabbing Moira's hand and walking up to meet him on the porch.

He picked Moira up and held her close, squeezing his eyes closed as though to keep the tears from falling. "There's my sweet girl!"

"Daddy!" Moira nestled her face against his and held him tight around the neck.

Dylan looked at me helplessly. He still wore his tux, though hopelessly wrinkled, the necktie hanging loose from his collar. He smiled a small, crooked smile as he squeezed her as close as he could. It struck me how truly good and genuine he was, and I felt ashamed.

I had kept so much a secret from him and accepted his proposal without truly giving him my entire heart. I couldn't see how he would ever forgive me or trust me again.

"I thought you would be with S-a-m now," he whispered under his breath.

"No ... no, I mean ... no." I said, at a loss for words, feeling awkward. "He just ... I ..."

I took his hand and held it to my lips, marveling at its warmth and strength as I held it to me. The love I felt for him surged through me, and suddenly a swell of desperation overcame me. What happens if he doesn't want me now? What if he refuses to take me back?

I felt as though I was truly looking at him for the first time. I realized how wonderful and patient he had been for so long, holding me all those long nights, unknowingly putting my heart back together. I had held back giving him my entire heart because I was afraid he would leave me, like Sam had. But in doing so, I gave him no choice but to leave in the end.

He pulled his hand back, reluctantly.

"Maggie ..." Dylan was hesitant. "I know what I saw in

your eyes when you looked at him, and there was something there that I've never seen when you've looked at me. I adore you, but I also respect myself too much to ignore what I saw. I can't get the image of you and him out of my mind, and I think we should just take some time apart until you know for sure what you want. Until I know that I can trust this ... trust 'us'."

Moira looked at him, nose to nose. "So, you don't want me, neither?"

"No ... I mean yes, of course I want you, Moira, but ..." Dylan's voice caught in his throat. "I love you, and I love your Mommy very much, but Mommy and I need to take a little vacation from each other to sort things through."

"And after that, can we be together?" Moira's tiny voice was hopeful.

Dylan hugged her close, unable to speak.

"Okay," I said, nodding, a thick lump in my throat. "You're right. We should ... take a ... vacation from one another."

Dylan set Moira down gently and smiled through tears that refused to fall. "I'll see you soon, sweet girl."

"Okay, see you soon." Moira smiled sadly and went in for one last hug.

"Can I ask you for one favor? Will you please give me my rings back, and will you put yours back on? We're technically still married, and I do love you, even if we're going to take a ... vacation."

Dylan hesitated, then put his hand deep in his pocket and pulled out our rings. He slid them back on our fingers, first mine and then his own.

"For now, Maggie, but I can't promise ... forever."

I gulped, catching my breath. Forever had been what the day was supposed to be about, but now he didn't know, and it was my fault.

I looked at Dylan, not sure if I should try to hug him. I wanted him to hold me so badly, but I knew he was hurt and angry, and I couldn't blame him. I was hurt and angry, too. All the healing I had done to convince myself I no longer loved or needed Sam had been destroyed in one moment. I dug my nails into my palm in frustration as I tried to hold back the hot, angry tears. I didn't want to cry in front of Dylan because part of me knew it was selfish, while the other part of me knew he couldn't stand to see me in pain.

Manipulating him through my tears would be wrong, so I took a deep breath and tried to force a smile.

"When will we talk?" I asked, my voice shaky.

"I don't know, Maggie. Let's just give it some time." Dylan reached out as though to touch my cheek, but pulled back just before he made contact.

I nodded, afraid to open my mouth for fear that I would beg him to forgive me and take me back, making a complete fool out of myself. I knew in my heart that Dylan was wise to take a step back. He knew what I knew, that Sam had an effect on me that I wasn't prepared to deal with quite yet. I also knew with complete certainty that I absolutely did not want to lose Dylan.

As we said good-bye I lingered, waiting for him to stop me but knowing that he wouldn't. As Moira and I walked away, I had a sinking feeling that it might just be too late.

THE NEXT FEW DAYS WERE LONELY AND DEVASTATING. THE days we were supposed to be on our honeymoon, I sat in my apartment instead, staring at numerous packed boxes and wondering what I should do with them.

Unpack them? Leave them? Unpack them?

Instead, Moira and I cuddled up and watched one Disney

movie after another. I cried until I had no more tears as I watched the beautiful princesses getting their happily ever afters.

"Mommy, why are you crying?" Moira kept asking, touching my face and clearly worried.

"Mommy is okay, Moo." I hugged her hard, unsure if I was trying to reassure myself or her.

Sam called on the third day.

"Mags?" His voice was raspy and soft, and inwardly I thrilled at the sound of it like I always did.

"Sam." I tried to ignore the deep timbre of his voice that always affected me so strongly. It was deeply familiar, warming me from within.

"I'm sorry I haven't called. I wanted to give you a few days because I wasn't sure if you would be pissed at me. I didn't know if you'd even want to talk to me at all." His voice was hesitant. "I just can't ... can't stop thinking about ... you ... and meeting Moira, and I had to call."

"Okay," I said, quietly.

"You're not ... on your honeymoon?" Sam spoke carefully.

"No," I pushed down a sob. "I'm not."

"I'm sorry, Mags. I'm so, so sorry. I didn't mean to ruin things for you, I swear." He sounded genuinely sorry.

"It's not your fault. I just didn't ... I didn't react very well to seeing you, and I should have told Dyl about you, but I never did. I kept you to myself instead, which was wrong. All of this has been so wrong."

I knew what I had done by burying my life with Sam, and hurting Dylan was the worst of it.

There was silence on the other end. I knew Sam was trying to figure out what to say next.

"I ... I would like to meet Moira, if I could," Sam said, his voice so quiet I could barely hear him.

"Yes. I would like that, too." I responded a little too

quickly, but I had been waiting all of Moira's life for her to meet Sam. While I had accepted that Sam and I may never be together, I wanted Moira to know him. I knew deep down that he would love her, and that she would love him. "What about Julie? Would Julie like to meet her? I just know that Julie would love her."

Sam was silent for so long that I wondered if he was still there. Just as I was about to ask if he was still there, he spoke.

"Mom died, Mags. It's been almost three years now."

I gasped, the wind knocked out of me. "Oh, God ... I'm so sorry, Sam. What happened?"

Sam cleared his throat and spoke slowly. "She ... she ... stopped taking her medication and she ... tried to commit suicide again. This time I wasn't there to save her."

My chest ached, thinking of all the times she called me "sweetie" and how kind she had always been to me, even when my own mother had not been. I knew how devastated Sam must have been.

"I'm so ... sorry." I wasn't sure what else to say. I knew there were no words that could comfort him or soothe his pain.

"There is something you should know ... something I want you to know, but I don't want you to hate me more than you already do, and I'm sure you will." Sam's voice was hesitant.

My heart stopped. I wasn't sure that I could possibly endure any more. My heart felt as though it had so many cracks in it, any more pressure would cause it to break into a thousand pieces.

"I don't know that I want to know, Sam," I said, gripping the phone.

"I'm sorry ..." Sam was silent as though reading my anticipation.

"Just ... tell me ..." I said, clenching my jaw and bracing myself for anything.

"I want to meet Moira. I want to know her ... and I want her to know me and my fiancée." Sam's voice trailed off softly.

My ears began to ring.

His fiancée? The pounding in my head began slowly and quietly, until it became so loud that I couldn't hear anything but the steady thump of my heart.

"Mags? Mags? Are you okay?" Sam's voice rang in my ears. Of course he had forgotten all about me and moved on! I had never meant anything to him after all. I should have known. He hadn't given me a choice but to forget, but he'd had one all along. The anger welled up inside of me, tempered by heartache and disappointment, and I struggled to think.

"Yes, I'm here. I'm okay," I said, finally finding my voice.

"I wasn't sure how you would take the news. I'm sorry, I should have told you, but it didn't feel like the right time. When I saw you ... I ... just ... " He sounded as hurt as I felt.

"How long ... have you been engaged?" I couldn't find the words to ask the question that would tell me if he had forgotten about me immediately, or if it had taken him as long as it had taken me.

"A ... few years."

I breathed in sharply. Moira was five, which meant that he had moved on from our life together so quickly. The part of my heart that carried him for so long slowly began to wither away inside my chest, along with the love I had saved for him.

I was silent.

"Mags, are you okay?" Sam's voice was soft, and I ached at the sound of it.

"Yes," I said after a few long moments. "I'm okay."

"I suppose we should talk ... I should explain ... I never meant to hurt you, Mags." Sam's voice was pleading, twisting me up inside with every syllable and every breath.

"Yes," I said quietly, afraid that if I took too deep of a breath that I might break.

"Yes?" he asked, hesitantly.

"Yes ... you can meet Moira and introduce her to your ... fiancée."

We worked out the details, and I hung up the phone, my thoughts lingering on the sound of his voice and how it used to whisper in my ear every night, winding its way through me in my dreams.

I wondered if he missed me at all, and how he moved on so quickly. How could he have forgotten about me so easily, this man that had been my everything? He had been my entire world, and when he left, the bottom fell out and me with it, landing helplessly into a messy, putrid pile. The only thing that had kept me afloat was Moira, until Dylan came along and taught me how to love once again.

As I began to breathe normally, I was terrified as I realized that for the first time in a long time, I was completely lost.

"I'M SORRY FOR WHAT I'VE DONE TO YOU, MAGS. I'VE BEEN selfish and cruel. I don't know why we have this connection the way that we do. I don't know why I moved on without you. But everything has happened for a reason. I just hope I haven't hurt you too much."

Sam's voice came from Dylan's mouth.

I stared at him confused.

"You've never hurt me, Dylan. You've been nothing but good to me. I'm so sorry for what I've done to you. I should've let Sam go a long time ago, and none of this would've ever happened. I don't know why I held onto him for so long. I don't know why I never told you about him. I'm sorry, so, so very sorry."

Dylan looked at me, his eyes a mixture of sadness and pain behind his wire rimmed glasses. "It's not your fault. I did this to you."

"No! No, you didn't." I reached for him but he backed away from me.

"Yes, I did. I've loved you for so long and then I left you. I shouldn't have left you the way I did."

"Please ..." I kept reaching for him and he kept backing away. "Please... stay, Dylan. Please don't walk away. I'm sorry, I'll do anything."

"I'm only doing what I should have done a long time ago. I'm only doing this to avoid hurting you."

"No. Dylan ... stay. Don't leave me." Tears ran uncontrollably, the saltiness from my tears burning my lips.


THE DREAM ENDED, AND I AWOKE TO SUNLIGHT STREAMING into my room, my pillow soggy from my tears. I was finally able to let go of Sam, and now Dylan didn't know if he wanted to be with me anymore.

I suddenly felt an emotion deep in my bones that had been long-forgotten, and I realized that I was completely alone.

## ❧ 23 ❧

# PREPARING

# M aggie

THE DAY OF THE MEETING, I FIDGETED ALL MORNING.

I didn't tell my parents, though I couldn't help but want my mother with me for comfort. It was strange how I had never thought of her as being comforting, but as I grew older, I realized that I understood her so much more than I ever thought I would. I needed her steely brazenness and ability to keep up appearances even during the worst of times, now more than ever. I didn't want Sam or his nameless fiancée to see that I was falling apart. I didn't want the fear and shame of his rejection that I carried inside to escape from eyes.

"Where are we going, Mommy?" Moira asked, her aqua eyes that always made me see Sam dancing with the dimple in her right cheek.

"We're going to see ..." my voice failed, and I paused to

find my voice. She needed to see that I was happy and that I wanted this. She needed to know that I approved.

"See who, Mommy?" Moira's impatience always made me laugh, and this time was no different.

"We're going to see your ... daddy... Sam. He's wants to introduce you to his, um... fiancée." I said, finally.

"Oh," Moira said, her little brows weaving together. "Weren't you his finn-ancee?" she asked, simply.

I paused before I answered.

"Yes, at one time I was Sam's fiancée, but that was a long time ago." My mind flashed back to when Sam was on his knees before me, holding up the small but sparkly ring that I would later put back into the ring box and hide in the back corner of my drawer forever, only daring to pull it and all the memories that came with it out when I heard our song, or if I had too much wine.

I wondered how he'd met her, how he'd asked her, how they'd fallen in love. Did the sound of his voice crawl deep inside of her, or the touch of his fingertips leave an invisible imprint on her skin like it had on mine? Did his existence in her life give her life meaning and wonder? Did she love him as deeply and completely as I had, and did he love her the same?

How could he have forgotten me so quickly and with such finality?

"Mommy?"

A tug on my arm stopped the torrent of questions that wreaked havoc in my brain as I started, realizing that Moira was staring up at me, questioning.

"Are you okay?"

"Yes, Moo. I'm okay," I said, wiping my eyes briefly, hoping she didn't notice the tears that hadn't yet fallen.

"Should we go?" she asked, staring at the clock that she couldn't yet read.

"Yes," I said, sighing.

I gathered myself, taking a deep breath.

I want my mommy, I thought suddenly as I reached into my pocket and pulled out my phone.

"I'm surprised you called," my mother said, her hair perfectly in place as she arrived at my apartment in record time, polished and pretty as ever.

"I ... I don't know why, but I just ..." the words never flowed easily where she was concerned. Even though things were different between us now, I struggled to find the words to express the woman I had become instead of the girl I still felt I was in her presence.

"I know, Maggie. You don't have to say," she said, patting me awkwardly on the shoulder. She was trying to be more affectionate, and I could sense her discomfort but also her resolve. She smiled, and the genuineness of it warmed me.

"Thanks, Mom," I said, returning her smile

"Grandma!" Moira came rushing into the room running full force into her. My mom laughed, her composure gone and replaced with joy, which made her more beautiful than I had ever seen her. "Are you here to meet my daddy and his finn-ancee with us?

My mother laughed.

"Fiancée?" she asked, raising her eyebrow.

I nodded, tightening my lips, afraid I would say more.

She kept her eyes on me for a moment longer and then turned her attention to Moira.

"Yes, I am!" she said, stroking Moira's soft ringlets.

"Good," Moira said, grabbing her hand and dragging her toward the door. "We're late. Hurry Mommy, let's go."

"Okay," I sighed.

The drive to the coffee shop in town where we were

meeting was a short distance from our apartment. I had never been there, though I had passed by many times and meant to stop. I wasn't sure why he had chosen it. It seemed safe, though my heart was pounding wildly in my chest. Letting him go had been the most difficult thing I'd ever had to do, but this was coming close. I'd never shared Moira with anyone else, and even though Sam was her father, I had grown accustomed to the reality that he wasn't in her life and never would be.

I sat in the car, pausing for a long moment.

"Are you ready?" my mother asked, touching my arm lightly.

"Yes," I sighed.

"Let's go, Mommy!" I turned and looked at her, and for a moment all I could see in her beautiful face were reminders of Sam, and my heart sank.

I tried to erase the thought from my mind that I was about to lose her forever.

## ❧ 24 ❧

## THE MEETING

# M aggie

WE WALKED INTO THE COFFEE SHOP WHERE WE HAD agreed to meet, my heart nearly pounding out of my chest.

Moira was holding my hand tightly, our palms sweaty. I wasn't sure who was more nervous, me or her.

As we opened the door, the coffee shop seemed to expand, and as I searched the room for Sam, my heart sank.

He was sitting at a corner table, leaning in toward a woman whose back was to us. She looked strangely familiar from behind, her dark, unruly hair reminding me of someone long-forgotten.

I took a deep breath and squeezed Moira's hand.

She looked up at me and smiled.

"Everything is going to be okay, Mommy," she said, sounding much wiser than her years. "Daddy is going to take good care of me."

"Your daddy won't need to take care of you, Moo. You're just going to meet him. You're just ..." I pushed back the tears I could feel brimming in my eyes."

As I tried to walk toward them, suddenly my feet were frozen, and I was unable to move.

"Mommy? Are you okay?" Moira looked up at me with concern.

I nodded, fighting the panic as I fought to move my feet. No matter how hard I tried they refused to move.

"Margaret, are you okay?" My mother's hand was on my shoulder. I met her brown eyes with mine and wondered if she could see my fear.

I looked over at Sam and saw him stand up and walk toward us, Moira suddenly materializing in his arms.

Everything was moving in slow motion, and I realized that I wasn't breathing, wasn't moving.

The woman who was with Sam stood up and turned slowly toward me, and I felt my heart stop instantly.

As she looked at me, concern etched all over her pretty face, I recognized her immediately. Her hair was a warm brown, and her eyes were dark and liquid. Her lips were turned up in an easy smile as she walked toward me, her arms open for a hug that I didn't want to give. Sam looked at her with obvious adoration as he kept his hand on the small of her back.

I wanted to throw up. I wanted to run and scream as my mouth opened but no sound came out.

As she and Sam got closer, the nausea grew stronger, and as I stared at her in disbelief, confusion swirled around me like a whirlwind.

Sam's fiancée wasn't just anyone.

She was *me*.

## ❧ 25 ❧

# THE TRUTH

# S am

IT WAS EASIER FOR ME TO LET HER BELIEVE I DIDN'T LOVE her anymore than tell her the truth.

I had lain in the hospital bed after the car accident and realized that I was no good for her. It was as though nearly dying made me realize who I was. I had been faking it the entire time I was with her.

I was a piece of shit, and I didn't deserve her. She was an angel, and I was ... nothing. I'd never been anything even though I'd fooled myself into believing that I could change. I sent her away because she didn't know that the accident had been my fault, and I never wanted her to find out.

I'd been high.

I'd been high at the interview because I was high almost every day. I'd done a damn good job of hiding my addiction from her because I'd never wanted her to see that part of me. That half of me. I'd been addicted to one thing or another for as long as I could remember, and it had become my normal. The only time I didn't need to be high was when I was with her. She had become the drug I'd been looking for all along, but when I wasn't right next to her, I needed it to keep the pain away.

What she didn't understand is that I never would've left her. I loved her more than I'd ever imagined loving anyone, but then I was ashamed. I was ashamed of my past and the father who didn't love me enough to stay in my life. I hated the life I'd lived before I met her, filled with drugs, alcohol, women and an addict-mom, whose choices with men had scarred me. My life with Mags was a lie, fabricated to make her fall in love with me.

Then I ran, like my father. I became what I didn't want to be, and I even did it knowing she was pregnant. I had seen the test in the trash and knew she was waiting to tell me, but I was terrified of being a horrible father, afraid to fail, so I abandoned her and Moira in the worst way. I had planned to be alone forever, but after my mom relapsed and overdosed, I was a disaster.

That's when Lea found me, and as hard as I tried to love her as much as Mags, I couldn't. I wanted to, and even when I was close to her, our bodies moving together in perfect time, my mind always drifted. I could never forget how cruel and heartless I had been to the one person I had waited to find my entire life. I hated myself, convinced that I would never come back for her, but no matter how hard I tried, I couldn't stay away.

I DIDN'T KNOW WHY BUT I NEEDED HER TO KNOW THE truth. I don't know what I expected to happen. Would she take me back or forgive me? The best I could hope for would be that she might let me get to know Moira and be the father I had never imagined I could be.

## ❧ 26 ❧

# THE OTHER WOMAN

# M aggie

"HI, I'M LEA," A TALL BRUNETTE WITH DARK EYES SMILED as she put her hand out to me. The woman I thought was me wasn't me at all. She was someone else entirely, a version of me that I had recognized immediately. I stared at the resemblance, though nobody else seemed fazed by it.

"Hi, I'm ..."

"Mags," Lea said, cutting me off. "I know exactly who you are. Sam told me all about you."

I strained to smile, trying hard to dislike the girl who was standing in front of me but failing miserably. She was several years younger than me, and her smile was infectious.

"I'm happy to meet you," she said, genuinely. If the shoe had been on the other foot, I wondered if I would have been so gracious, but she had a kindness in her eyes that very few possessed.

"Me, too," I said, meaning it.

We all stood staring at one another, hesitant to make a move, ignoring the crowd moving around us as they struggled to find the line to order their coffees.

"Hi. I'm Moira," Moira said stepping forward and putting her hand out, waiting for Sam to shake it. His eyes welled up, a large smile taking over his still-handsome face.

"Hi Moira. I'm your ... I'm Sam."

"My dad," Moira said, matter-of-factly.

"Yes, your dad." Sam shuffled his feet, uncomfortable.

"Where have you been?" she asked, no judgment in her voice, only curiosity.

Sam cleared his throat, reddening as he looked at my mother.

"I've been ... I've ..."

"He's been lost," I said, picking her up and kissing her soft ringlets. "But he's here now, and that's all that matters."

I could feel his eyes on me, burning into me like they used to, and I tried to ignore the feelings that came barreling back.

"Okay, Mom-ee," Moira said, snuggling her head into my neck, not taking her eyes off Sam.

"Should we sit down?" Lea asked, pointing to a table and then taking everyone's order when we settled in. She bounced up to stand in line while we sat and stared at one another.

I was beginning to regret bringing my mother with us as she stared at Sam, her eyes full of scorn.

"So ... Moira, what types of things do you like?" Sam asked, trying to break the awkwardness.

The next hour was filled mostly with Moira's high staccato voice punctuated by giggles as she talked about her stuffed animals, her favorite television shows, foods and dolls. Sam listened intently, rarely taking his eyes off her even as Lea reappeared with his coffee that he barely touched.

Sam kept shaking his head in amazement, and I could see

the recognition in his eyes as he saw bits of himself in her, just as I had been doing her entire life.

As we were finishing up the visit, Sam was hesitant to walk toward the door as Lea grasped his hand, her small diamond ring flashing in the light. She caught me looking at it and looked embarrassed.

"Can I ..." Sam spoke slowly.

"You can see her anytime you want," I interrupted. "She's been waiting for you, and now that you're here, she's not going to lose you."

I paused, a pang of guilt hitting me. I knew I should only be talking about Moira, but I also knew that I referring to myself. I had been waiting for him. I didn't want to lose him again.

My mother caught my eyes as though reading my mind. She smiled, her eyes soft and warm, giving me immediate comfort.

I took a deep breath.

"Thank you," Sam said, reaching out toward me and then lowering his hand immediately. I was grateful that he pulled back. I knew that if he touched me I might not be able to mask my feelings, and I didn't want Lea to see how much Sam still affected me. I liked her, and didn't want to see her hurt.

I knew what Sam's absence could do and the emptiness that resulted. I didn't want her to experience the same.

"You're welcome," I said, avoiding his gaze. "Anytime."

## ✤ 27 ✤

# THE GOOD DOCTOR

# M aggie

THE NEXT DAY MY PHONE RANG AND I WAS STARTLED TO see that it was Dylan.

"Maggie." Dylan's voice was a welcome sound in my ear on the other line. It had been days since we'd spoken, and I had kept my distance like I'd promised even though it had been very difficult. I thought about him non-stop, my heart torn with my love for Dylan and feelings that had resurfaced for Sam. "Can we meet?"

"Yes," I said, relieved. I'd hated our last meeting, the thought of never seeing Dylan again breaking my heart.

"Can we meet alone?" he asked, hesitantly. He'd always included Moira in everything, so meeting without her troubled me.

"Sure," I said, wanting to say no instead.

We made arrangements to meet at the wine bar by his

house, a place we'd had one of our first dates, which I took as a good sign. My mother agreed to stay with Moira as I nervously readied myself, unsure of what to think.

Dylan had come into my life so unexpectedly and had been the first person since Sam to ever make me feel safe. A few men had asked me out over the years, but I'd always backed out until Dylan. He'd been different, and while he wasn't the most adventurous or free-spirited, he'd been someone I could trust.

Moira had taken to him immediately and called him DD until she could say "Daddy Dylan." He'd been hooked by her right away, smitten as most were from the moment he'd met her.

"After meeting her, I couldn't break up with you even if I wanted to," he'd joked many times. She'd wrapped him around her little finger, and he had taken good care of her.

I walked into the wine bar nervously, the sound of my heels echoing on the tile floor. It was dark in the bar. I waited for my eyes to adjust to the light before I could search the bar stools for Dylan.

"Maggie." I followed the sound of his voice and took a deep breath as I walked toward him.

"Hi," I said, suddenly feeling shy. He looked handsome in a crisp blue button-down shirt, his eyes bright behind his glasses.

"Hi yourself," he said, smiling. I'd always found his quiet confidence sexy, and suddenly he seemed irresistible.

I sat down, a glass of Cabernet already in front of me as I took a large gulp, nearly draining the entire glass.

Dylan looked at me, his eyes wide.

"It's your favorite," he said, taking a small sip of his Pinot Grigio and gesturing to the waitress for another glass for me as I quickly finished off my first one.

"Thank you," I said, the wine warming me as I felt myself

start to relax.

"You're welcome. How is Moira?" Dylan asked as he played with the stem of his glass. He was trying not to appear too eager, but I knew that he was dying to know.

"She's good, Dyl. She's just ... confused, but she's taking things in stride." I wasn't sure I should tell him about Sam.

As though reading my mind Dylan asked the next question he was dying to know the answer to. "What about ... Sam?"

The question hung heavy in the air between us.

"Moira met him." I plunged right in knowing that I couldn't avoid it. Dylan took a sharp breath.

"What? How?" he asked, unable to form a complete sentence, his usually calm demeanor thrown off by the news.

"He called and wanted to meet her, so we met him and his fiancée..."

"Fiancée?" Dylan's ears perked up.

"Yes," I said repeating the word as though I needed to say it again for myself. "Fiancée."

"Wow, that guy is just full of surprises, isn't he?" Dylan said, draining his glass and gesturing for the waitress to bring him another.

"She's very nice," I said, feeling it necessary to be complimentary. "And pretty."

"Surely not as pretty as you are," Dylan said, his cheeks a little pink from the wine.

Wine made him happy and relaxed, and I loved seeing that side of the otherwise-reserved him.

"I guess that depends on what you consider pretty," I said, smiling.

Dylan reached across the table for my left hand, touching the diamond ring.

"You didn't take it off?" he asked, his voice thick with emotion.

"No, of course not," I said, placing my hand on his. "I wasn't going to take it off until you told me to."

Dylan looked at me, tears welling up in his eyes. "I thought for sure you were going to leave me for him. When I saw you together, I knew that what you had with him was something ... "

"Different. It was different than what you and I have, Dyl, but I love you. You've been good to me, and I adore you."

Before I could react, Dylan's lips were on mine, possessive and fierce, kissing me in a way he'd never done before. I could taste the wine on his tongue as his hands roamed over me, needing me as much as I needed him.

He hurriedly paid the tab and we left, barely able to get out the door before he pushed me up against the wall, his body melting against mine, hard and wanting.

The short drive back to his house was torture, and as he carried me up the stairs to the bedroom, our clothes falling as we peeled them off of one another, I lost myself completely in him.

He took me with a passion that I'd never experienced with him, as though he'd suddenly been possessed. His thrusts were harder and deeper than I remembered, his fingers leaving marks on my skin where he'd otherwise been far gentler. I could barely catch my breath as he took me over and over.

When we'd had our fill of one another, we lay panting, our sweaty limbs entwined, both of us too spent to move. I couldn't remember feeling this way in so many years as I felt myself slip into a restful and contented sleep, my mind blank.

"I love you, Maggie." A warm voice filled my ear as I smiled, snuggling up against him, enjoying the feel of his naked skin on mine.

"I love you too," I said dreamily. "I always have and I always will ... Sam."

## ✤ 28 ✤

## THE OTHER HALF OF ME

S am

I'M IN LOVE.

Moira is perfect and everything I'd ever imagined her to be, from the top of her curly head to the bottom of her cute toes and everything in between.

Seeing her makes me realize how much of her life I missed, and I'm full of regret. I know that I'll never get that time back, and I'm nearly overcome with so much grief because of it.

I don't know how I ever could've left her or Mags. I'm my father. I know it. I'd always known I would turn into him.

The difference is that I've come back, and I'm going to change things. I'm going to make up for everything I've done, or I'm going to die trying.

I need to get them back, but I don't know how they'll

ever forgive me. How will they get past me leaving them? How will they ever understand, and how will Lea understand? With her help, I've been clean and sober for several years, but I don't love her like I love Mags. Even though I've tried to convince her, I know she doesn't believe me because I can see the doubt in her beautiful dark eyes. Yet for some reason, she stays with me, never complaining, always cheerful, and I want to love her so badly.

I know that I don't deserve her. I've never deserved anyone to love me, but somehow it still finds me.

I wouldn't be surprised if Mags hated me forever, but I know that she wouldn't. She doesn't have that kind heart to hate, though most would.

The thought that I've lost her completely plagues me night and day, and I know that even if she stays married to this other guy, that I'll have deserved an entire lifetime of emptiness and regret without her. I know that I'll have to let Lea go to move on with her life because it wouldn't be fair to keep her imprisoned in my own selfishness. A lifetime alone, with Moira, who reminds me so much of my mom and all I've lost, is all I'll ever deserve in this life.

Deep down inside, when I look in the mirror I know that I don't even deserve that.

※

MAGGIE

I SAT IN THE MIDDLE OF MY APARTMENT, BOXING UP OUR wedding gifts and printing up address labels.

I had finally managed to put everything back in its rightful place, unpacking mine and Moira's lives from the boxes that had been meant to join Dylan's.

I looked down at my empty ring finger and sighed. Things should have been different between us, and I thought they might be after our date at the wine bar, but Sam's name had escaped my lips, breaking Dylan's heart.

While I slept fitfully, Dylan paced all night, and when I awoke, I was met with his red puffy eyes and exhausted face.

"I've been trying to figure out how to say this to you, Maggie," he'd blurted out before my eyes were even completely open.

"Dyl ... what... can I have some coffee first? Are you okay?" I rubbed my eyes furiously, trying to wake up.

"No! I mean ... can you just listen to me?" he asked, his voice cracking.

I sat up, swinging my legs over the bed to face him in the chair he was sitting in.

"You said his name" Dylan said, the words not making any sense.

"What do you mean?" I asked, my mind racing back to what I'd said to him the previous night. "Whose name?"

"Sam. You said it. You said that you loved me forever and always, but you weren't really saying it to me, you were saying it to Sam. You said Sam." He was speaking quickly as I tried desperately to follow.

" I don't ... I didn't ..." I'd said his name so many times, I wondered if it was true.

"I'm not making it up, Maggie. Believe me, if I could pretend you'd never said it I would, but I can't. I heard it, and I know that if we stay together, you'll say it again, and I just can't wait for that to happen. I thought that if I loved you enough ... if you loved me at all that I could be okay with this, but I can't. I can't be okay with you loving someone else."

I sat in silence, tears forming and sliding down my cheeks before I could stop them. I knew that I must have said it, and that it must be true, and I was ashamed. How could I have hurt him like that?

"I'm sorry, Dyl. I didn't mean to say his name. I would never do that do you." I shook my head, wondering how I could've slipped like that.

"It's not your fault, Maggie. I know you didn't mean to hurt me, but I won't love somebody who loves someone else. You need to be honest with yourself and deal with this."

I nodded, reaching for him as we fell into each other's arms. I felt as though my heart was ripping apart and I refused to let him go. We held onto one another for what felt like hours, but I knew that when I looked back on it, it wouldn't have felt like long enough.

Loving him had helped heal me, and losing him felt wrong, but I understood that he deserved so much more. Parting was like ripping off a layer of skin, but we finally let go, and I had to break the news to Moira.

"So, I'll never see Daddy Dylan ever again?" she'd cried in my arms.

"He wants to still see you, Moo, but we won't be married anymore. I'm sorry," I said, drying her tears.

"But don't you love each other?" She asked, her simple logic making me feel stupid.

"Yes, we do, but it takes more than that to be married." My heart ached for her. Dylan had been the closest thing to a father she'd ever known, and she loved him. Ripping him out of her life was unforgivable, and I knew that I would carry the guilt with me for the rest of my life.

"Is it because of Sam?" Moira had refused to call him anything but Sam since the coffee shop, and I didn't force her to call him Daddy. He had only just appeared in her life, and she needed to be comfortable to accept him.

"Yes ... no ... it's because of a lot of things, Moo. It's not just Sam."

"Oh." Moira left the room and reappeared a few moments later with a stuffed dog that Dylan had given her.

"I'm keeping Max with me," she said simply.

"That's a good idea," I said, kissing her on the forehead. "I really am so sorry, Moo."

"I know Mommy. But I'm mad at you."

## ❧ 29 ❧
# THE VISIT

# M aggie

MOIRA WAS DISTRAUGHT FOR DAYS, BUT AS OUR APARTMENT became more like home, she began to settle back in, and our life reverted back to a new normal without Dylan. We both missed him as we moped around, avoiding mentioning his name but keeping Max with us as a reminder of him everywhere we went.

As I stood in the middle of the boxes, finally finished with the wedding gifts, my back aching from kneeling on the floor, there was an unexpected knock on the door that startled me.

"I got it!" Moira yelled, running toward the door. I shooed her away, getting there first. I'd been teaching her never to answer the door, but she was a girl with a mind of her own.

I opened the door, her hands clutching my legs, and was shocked to see Sam standing there. For a long moment, I was frozen as we stood staring at one another.

"Hi," I said, finally finding my voice.

"Hi." His voice was rough, making my heart rate speed up against my will. I opened the door a little wider, allowing him to enter.

"Hi, Moo," he said, bending down to tweak Moira's nose. She pulled away angrily, never letting anyone touch her nose without permission.

"No, Sam!" she said, swatting his hand away with Max. "Only Mommy, Daddy Dylan and Grandma call me Moo. You call me Moira."

Sam looked hurt but pulled back.

"Okay, I'm sorry."

Moira turned and bounced away without saying a word.

"Is she okay?" Sam asked, flustered. Moira had responded well to him in the coffee shop, but was angry with him now.

"She's fine, but she's upset that Dyl and I aren't staying married. She asked me if it was your fault."

Sam raised his eyebrows, but didn't say anything.

He looked around, surveying the wreckage of boxes, labels, and packing tape.

"Do you need help?" he asked, changing the subject.

"No, I'm done." I was irritated as I picked up boxes and stacked them by the door to take to the post office.

"I can help you ..."

"I said no!" I told him forcefully.

"Maybe I should leave," Sam said edging toward the door.

"No, it's fine. I'm sorry. It's been a rough few days, and Moo ... Moira and I are settling back into a new routine. Please, stay. We can order pizza and start over." I knew that we were being unfair to Sam, blaming him for missing Dylan, but it wasn't his fault entirely. I knew that even if Moira didn't.

"Pizza!" Moira came flying into the room, her tutu

floating behind her as she crashed into Sam, her earlier frustration forgotten.

I smiled at Sam. "Life with a five-year-old," I said simply.

He picked her up cautiously and carried her around as Moira introduced him to Max. He listened intently, hanging on her every word.

The evening was uneventful as we ate our pizza and watched a movie, Moira crashing on the couch between us, Max snuggled firmly in her arms.

"May I?" Sam asked nodding to Moira.

"Yes," I said leading him to her bedroom where he put her down gently, kissed her forehead, and then covered her with a blanket. As he walked out of her room, he rubbed his eyes, embarrassed as he saw me staring at him.

"I've always wanted to do that," he said sheepishly.

I went in and kissed her softly. "Good-night, Moo," I whispered careful not to wake her.

We sat back on the couch, the mood in the room changing without Moira there.

"Can I ask you a question?" Sam asked after a few moments of silence.

"Sure," I ran my fingers through my hair, exhaustion taking over.

"Was it my fault?" he asked, thoughtfully.

"Was what your fault?"

"You and Dylan deciding not to be married," he said, revisiting our earlier conversation that I had forgotten.

I sighed.

"It doesn't matter now, Sam. Our lives are different, and you're engaged. I'm happy you can come here and put Moira to bed and that you and I can be in the same room, but my relationship with Dyl is none of your business. In fact, my life is none of your business." I struggled to keep my voice down as all of the pain and exhaustion of the past few weeks came to a head. I felt the anger well up inside of me. "You let me raise Moira alone for the first five years of her life and want to come back and play daddy now, but let's face it, you abandoned me. I trusted you the most, and you threw me away as though I never mattered."

Sam looked as though I had just slapped him, his face red as he took a step back.

"I know what I did, Mags. I know that I hurt you. I was going to come back, but then my mom went off the rails from the stress of my accident and stopped taking her meds. I should've come back and told you that she began taking drugs again, but I had to do everything I could to keep her off of them. The biggest thing I had to do Mags was clean myself up."

I registered what he was saying. "What do you mean, you had to clean up?"

Sam was quiet as he avoided my eyes.

"For a long time, I was an addict, Mags. I was trying hard to make something of myself when I met you, but with the pressure of trying to find a job, I just … I was weak and I reverted to my old ways. I was high when I had the accident and had to pay the consequences for that. Being an addict is the blame for every other failure in my life, including our relationship. It's how I eventually met Lea. She tried like hell to help my mom and has helped me stay clean. For that, I'll forever be indebted to her … but she let me go a few days ago because she saw how I still feel about you as much as I've tried to hide it. She could see it the moment that she met you."

My mind was reeling as I tried to understand what Sam was saying.

"You were an addict? When? Why didn't I ever see it?" I asked in disbelief.

"I hid it well, Mags. I was one for a lot of my life and good

at not letting you see it. When money and jewelry disappeared, you just assumed you'd lost it. When I was high, you
thought I was really happy, or sick, or just tired, and my mom
covered up for me when we thought you might suspect. It
was a dishonest life. The only thing I gave you that was true
was the ring I asked you to marry me with and my love. The
rest of it was a bullshit lie, and I'm so damned sorry."

Sam's confession knocked the wind out of me as I sank to
the ground.

"Why ... why have you come back now?" I asked weakly,
trying to understand it. "Why are you telling me all of this?"

"I ... I was hoping for forgiveness. Redemption? I was
hoping that when you knew the truth that you would tell me
that it didn't matter and that you loved me anyway. I was
hoping that I was still the other half of you and that despite
it all, I was still in your heart."

The atmosphere between us was thick, his words hanging
in the air.

"It's like I don't even know you anymore," I said angrily. "I
feel like our entire relationship was a lie."

"No, Mags. I swear, I was just messed up, but I'm better
now. I promise, please. Losing my mom made me see how
much I have to lose ... how much I've already lost. The pills
and alcohol and everything else are all done with. I'm clean
now and have been for several years. I never would've come
back to you if I wasn't."

"Please, Sam, just leave," I said, exhausted. "I can't do this
with you right now."

"Please, Mags. I'm begging you ..."

"Sam, I have a lot to think about because it's not just
about me. I have to think about Moira ..." I walked to the
door and opened it. "Please just go."

Sam walked to the door, his shoulders slumped in defeat.
A flash of him as a young boy and then as the man I fell in

love with nearly knocked me over, but I knew that I needed to let him go. I needed to think with my head and not my heart, and I needed to decide if I could live without him after I'd finally gotten him back in my life.

"Sam, I just need time ... and space. I need to think. Please, just let me do this," I pleaded.

He moved in closer, his breath on my ear as he leaned in.

"I'm still the same Sam, Mags. The difference is, you know my flaws now and the very worst of me. I'm not perfect, but I'll do anything to deserve your love and forgiveness and to have the chance to be Moira'a dad. Please."

He kissed me on the temple and walked out, the tears kept at bay until the door closed behind him.

My brain was a swirling torrent of emotions, and I knew that I would never be able to understand it all on my own. Immediately, I called the one person in my life who I knew would be able to pick it apart and put it back together for me so that it all made sense. She was the most flawed person I knew, but also the one who had taught me the most about redemption and forgiveness, and I needed that more than anything if l was ever going to get through this.

"Hello, Mom?"

## ❧ 30 ❧

# FORGIVENESS

# M aggie

FORGIVENESS WAS FOREIGN TO ME. I'D NEVER HAD TO forgive anyone until my mother, and I knew that I would never forgive Trip. Otherwise, there hadn't been many people in my life who needed forgiving. My mother was the first and only person who taught me the power of forgiving someone.

Until Moira came along, I always felt that I was either a major disappointment to her or inconvenience.

She had been hard on me as a child, bordering on cruel at times, making subtle yet hurtful comments about my appearance or a fault in my character. She was never happy with me and made sure I knew it. She blamed her sharp words on her mother who had been the same way, but I didn't care about fault. I just knew that she made me cry myself to sleep at night, as a child and an adult. Her words were like poison, and

I always thought that if she been as free with her love, my childhood might have been filled with confidence and friendship. Instead it was lonely and awkward, a miserable existence.

I even blamed her for Trip, but I knew deep down that it wasn't her fault entirely. While it would've been easy to blame her for everything that had gone wrong in my life, not everything could be blamed on her.

When Sam appeared and began to heal me, I finally understood that I had choices of my own to make. Sam's love allowed me to let go of my anger but also to be cautious. He taught me that I was lovable and worthy, something I'd never learned from her.

But it wasn't until Moira arrived that things between us changed completely. My mother was the only person that I knew in the room with me, and the moment Moira's dark head appeared, something inside of her changed. I watched, mesmerized as her brown eyes filled with tears, and her face transformed with sheer joy. She was filled with a happiness that I had never seen in her, and she glowed in the role of grandmother, though she had paled as a mother.

I fought my own jealousy for Moira's sake, wrecked that I had never invoked that level of joy in her. I reminded myself that my sweet girl didn't know that my childhood had been devoid of my mother's love, and I knew that my selfishness could never outweigh her happiness.

Moira adored her grandmother, and for the first time, I saw my mother act silly, make funny faces, dance and sing. She would do anything to make Moira smile, and in turn, I softened toward her, unable to stop myself. Because of her love for Moira, my heart could no longer hold onto the anger and resentment I had been carrying toward her for so long.

When Moira was three, my mother suddenly apologized,

blurting out the words as though they had been held captive inside of her for a long time. "I'm so sorry, Maggie!"

I had been waiting for her to apologize my entire life, always wondering if her regret would ever ease the pain of a childhood spent deprived of my mother's love. I'd assumed I would have to wait until her deathbed, or possibly never, and was surprised.

"I know that I wasn't a very good mother to you, and I'm sorry. I didn't realize how hurtful I was, but I do now because I can't imagine you ever saying the things I've said to Moira. I promise I'll be better," she said, shameful tears filling her eyes.

"Thank you, Mom. That means a lot to me, and I forgive you. Let's just put it behind us." I needed her far more than either of us ever realized, and so did Moira.

When I called her after Sam left, she came over immediately. We'd become comfortable in an unspoken rhythm of mother and daughter, not needing many words to explain what we meant or wanted from each other. We had bridged much in a short time, and I was grateful.

"Are you okay?" she'd asked after kissing Moira and settling her into bed for the night. I knew that she already knew the answer.

"Sam wants to come back ..." I said slowly.

"Do you want him back?" Her question caught me off-guard. I'd expected her to scoff or go off on a rant, but I hadn't expected her to ask me what I wanted.

"I don't know," I admitted. "I've lost Dyl for good, and I can't blame him. He deserves so much more, but Sam ..."

"Do you love him?" Mom asked, her eyes strangely soft in the light. She looked almost vulnerable, and I couldn't remember ever seeing her that way.

"I ... do ... I mean, I think I do. To be truthful, I've never stopped loving him, but he abandoned us. He left me alone when I was pregnant and didn't care what happened. I always thought that we were meant for one another ... that we were soul mates." I took a deep breath not sure if I should tell her everything. I had never told her everything before, and I was teetering on the precipice of the unknown. Our relationship felt new and old at the same time, but I wasn't sure how solid it was yet.

"There's more ..." she prodded, nodding ever so slightly.

"Yes," I said, trying not to sound as anxious as I felt, waiting for the judgement that would surely come after. "He just told me that ... when we were together ... he lied and stole from me. He was abusing pills and alcohol and was so good at hiding it that I never even knew it was happening right in front of me. I don't even know if I can trust him." I spoke quickly, afraid of what she would say and what she would think of me for even thinking about it.

She sat quietly with her eyes looking at her empty teacup, deep in thought. I had never seen her so quiet as I tried to calm my nerves and wait for the condemnation that was sure to follow.

"Do you have something a little stronger than this?" she asked, taking me by surprise.

"Uh ... sure, I have wine ..."

"Pour us a glass," she said, taking a deep breath.

I poured our wine and handed it to her, watching carefully as she took a long sip, then slowly began talking.

"I never wanted you to know this ..." she cleared her throat, finally looking up at me. "I've been ashamed all of these years, but you need to know now. I know that I focused on perfection with you as a child, but it was only because my life was far from perfect." She looked down at her fingers as though she could find the words to say written on them. "Your dad ... left me. You were only two when it happened ... too young to remember but ... he left because he was an addict, even though they didn't label it like they do now. It was misunderstood then, and people weren't as open and supportive about it. It was ugly, and even now he won't talk about it."

My mind was reeling.

My entire life I thought he gave my mother her way because he was weak, but was it shame? Was his obedience regret instead?

"How ... why ..." the questions were racing through my mind.

"He struggled his entire life. Alcohol, drugs, anything that took his mind from the pain of ... well his childhood was terrible, to say the least. Far worse than we ever told you. When I met him he was simply medicating, but as time when on it got worse. When I found out that I was pregnant with you I gave him a choice. Either the drugs or his family. When you were two he chose the drugs. He was gone for over a year, but he never stopped visiting you. You were his touchstone, and the only thing that kept him grounded."

I thought about Sam and how he looked at Moira, and I imagined my dad doing the same to me as a wave of emotion overcame me, and I fought back the tears.

"Eventually, he came back, and we worked things through, but it took many, many years. There was a lot of anger and resentment, but we kept it to ourselves because those are things you never spoke of. I was raised to keep up appearances, which meant that nobody could ever truly know what was going on inside."

My mother wiped her eyes with a tissue she had dug out of her pocket, tears escaping from her eyes against her will. I marveled at her strength, never understanding her before. I realized how little I knew of her pain and suddenly felt guilty for assuming that I knew her when I didn't. She had been hardened as a means to survive. She was human and imperfect, and in a strange way she had been trying to protect me.

"Why ... did you let him come back?" I asked, afraid of her answer. I couldn't imagine a life without my father, but suddenly understanding how raw and human he truly was made me feel a vulnerability I never had before, even when I was at my weakest. He had left us just as Sam did, and returned as Sam did as well.

My mother sniffled hard, her eyes clouding over for a moment, lost.

"I let him come back because I loved him and could never imagine my life without him, but it made me hard, especially toward you. I was angry because he came back for you, and not for me, so I wasn't always kind toward you, and I'll never forgive myself for that."

I hugged her hard, a gesture I never would've dared try a year before. She welcomed it as we held one another and cried.

"It's not as black and white as you think with Sam." She said eventually drying her eyes. "That boy still loves you and you love him."

It was a statement, not a question.

" I do," I said, admitting it to myself out loud. "I've never stopped loving him, and I've never been able to imagine a life without him, even though I did love Dyl. It just wasn't the same. Loving Sam was ... is ... like loving the deepest part of myself. We're connected in a way that I can't explain, and life without him has been hell."

"Then you know what you have to do, Maggie." My mother grabbed my hands and pulled me close to her. "You have to forgive that boy and allow him to spend every day of his life making it up to you."

I closed my eyes and fell into her arms exhausted as I sobbed against her shoulder. As she smoothed my hair and rocked me, I felt peace overcome me for the first time in a long time.

I finally knew after years of torment what I needed to do and could feel the strength welling up inside of me ready to do it.

## 31

# CONFESSION

S am

IT WAS LATE WHEN MY DOORBELL RANG, SCARING THE HELL out of me.

I wasn't expecting any visitors as I looked around my scant apartment for something to use as a weapon. I was living back in one of the many old apartments that I had shared with my mom, and even though I had a decent job with a steady paycheck, being there made me feel close to her, and I needed that after what I'd done to her. The neighborhood wasn't that great when we lived here and was even sketchier so many years later. I laughed at my cautiousness and took a deep breath to settle the thumping in my chest.

The doorbell rang again multiple times, and I opened the door ready to take on whatever was on the other side.

Mags!

I pulled her in swiftly, closing and locking the door behind her in one easy motion.

"Mags, what are you doing here so late?" I scolded, enjoying the look of shock in her pretty dark eyes.

She looked stunned and took a moment to collect herself.

"I ... U-u-uh needed to talk to you, and it couldn't wait," she said speaking quickly, her voice quivering.

"Where is Moira? Is she okay?" I asked worried.

"My mom is with her," she said taking a deep breath.

"Uh ... do you want something to drink? I have pop and tea. Sorry, nothing harder than that," I said squirming a little.

"No thanks," she said a little smile playing on her lips. I stared at her lips, a sudden urge coming over me to kiss them, but I tried to think of something else. She'd always been able to read my mind, and I didn't want her to read the thoughts I was having about her. So much had changed and passed between us, but when we were together it was as though nothing had changed between us at all.

I imagined that I could read her thoughts, too, but she was carefully hiding from me and I was curious.

"Okay, so why the late night visit?" I asked, not sure if I wanted the answer.

"Can we sit?" she asked, not waiting for permission as she sat down on the couch next to Cassie the cat, who had adopted me. I wasn't a cat person and preferred dogs, but Cassie had found me. She had been at her worst, bedraggled and starving, and I didn't have the heart to let her go, so I took her in and nursed her back to health. She thanked me by getting in the way and sticking her paws in my coffee cup every morning before I was half-awake. I hated her and loved her at the same time, and at the moment she was loving Mags.

Good choice, cat.

"Okay, the suspense is killing me. What's going on?" I

asked, turning toward her, aware that her knee was only a half an inch from mine. Being close to her made me feel drunk, which I'd always loved about her. She had been the only drug I'd ever needed until I messed everything up, and I was certain she had come to tell me to stay away from her and Moira forever.

I choked up inside. The thought of losing Moira gave me a sharp pain in my chest. I couldn't ever imagine loving a tiny person like her any more than I already did, even though I knew that I didn't deserve anything. I had missed so much ... the thought of missing more would kill me.

"What happened with Julie?"

The question threw me off guard.

I closed my eyes and put my head in my hands, running them through my hair repeatedly. I'd never wanted to tell Mags about Mom, but I didn't have a choice. I needed to tell her. I needed her to know that I hadn't stayed away because I didn't love her. I stayed away because I wanted to protect her from seeing what Mom had become.

"You don't want to know, Mags," I said, trying to dissuade her from finding out the awful truth. I had spared her for so long, and she had only ever known the wonderful side of my mom, because that's all we ever showed her. Mom had begged me not to ever tell Mags the truth, and I'd promised her.

"I need to know. I know that you weren't entirely truthful with me when you said she killed herself and that there's more. I know that you've never been one-hundred percent truthful with me, and I can't trust you unless I know that you've told me everything." Mags searched my eyes with hers, and I could feel myself falling under her spell. She had an effect on me that nobody else ever had, and as hard as I tried to look away from her, I was captivated.

She was even more beautiful now than she'd been when we'd met. She had rounded out and softened up in places where she'd been more sharp and angular, her body belonging to a woman, not a girl. I wanted so much to touch her, but I knew that she would push me away. I might have been able to distract her before, but not now. She was stronger and I was smitten.

"Start talking," Mags said, her voice commanding, but her eyes soft.

I cleared my throat and whispered for forgiveness.

"You knew my mom in the best years of her life," I said slowly, picturing her face when I'd first told her about Mags and me, and how proud she had been of me for finding a nice girl. "There were very few good years, and you saw most of them."

Mags gulped, her knee falling over to touch mine.

"She'd been abused as a child by a family friend, and then by her father, so she turned to drugs at an early age. When she was married to my dad, she had cleaned up, but she began drinking and was drinking pretty heavily when he left her. A lot of the time she didn't even know who she was or what was going on. She rarely remembered hitting me until she sobered up and saw the bruises she'd left behind, but I loved her, Mags. I did. I'd have done anything to protect her even though nothing I did could ever erase her pain."

Mags whimpered and grabbed my hands in hers as she pulled me closer.

"She tried many times to sober up. She'd quit the drugs and the alcohol, she'd go to church, she'd get a job, and then something would happen, and she would spiral at a moment's notice, and we'd go through it all over again. She made terrible choices in men, and when I got bigger, she never touched me again but the men in her life did, leaving even bigger bruises than she ever did. I tried running away a few times, but I always came back, knowing I could never leave her." I took a ragged breath, willing myself to have the strength to finish telling her. "When I met you, Mags, I thought that everything would change for me. I thought that I could be someone different, but without realizing it, I had become her and hid it from you. I tried to pretend that I was someone else, and you made me want to be, but I just couldn't do it."

"Why didn't you ever tell me?" Mags said, choking back a sob as she clutched my hands tightly. "Why did you hide it from me for so long? Didn't you trust me? I would've protected you."

"I couldn't," I said, standing up and pacing the room, tears fighting their way down my cheeks. "I had never told anyone, and I was the only person in her life left to protect her. I loved her, Mags. She was my mother, and nothing she could ever do to me would've made me abandon her. I just couldn't. We were all we'd ever had, and we needed one another."

Mags buried her head in her hands and sobbed, her entire body shaking. She'd loved my mom more than she'd loved her own at times, and I knew that it was breaking her heart.

"Why did she kill herself?" Her voice was muffled but her question was clear.

"She was tired, Mags. She'd been fighting her entire life, and my car accident had destroyed her resolve. I didn't tell them that I was an addict, so they gave me pain medication that I happily shared with her. We were toxic, but I'd have done anything to ease her pain. She finally spiraled out of control and when she did, she was angry and bitter, and she blamed me for everything even though I knew she knew better. In the end I was only trying to ease her pain, but I know that I contributed to her death. I don't know that I can ever forgive myself for that."

"I'm so sorry that you had to go through all of this, and that you had to do it alone," Mags stood up and hugged me, holding me tighter than I had ever remembered her doing before. "I'm sorry you didn't trust me with your pain. I'd have protected you from it like you did with mine. I'd have taken it from you."

"It wasn't your fault at all, Mags. It was mine alone, and I'm so sorry that I hurt you." The tears were relentless as they flowed, but with her I wasn't ashamed. She needed those tears to see that I was truly sorry for hurting her so badly. I'd convinced myself that she wasn't the one I had been dreaming about my entire life because I'd buried my love for her so deep that I'd forgotten that I could never be complete without her.

I had wanted to hold her from the moment I saw her again, and I pulled her in hard against me, our bodies tight, my hands roaming down her back full of want and desire. She looked me in the eye, and in a second, my mouth was crashing onto hers as I nearly explode with desire.

I could taste her salty tears as I consumed her lips with mine, my tongue exploring hers, enthralled by both the newness and familiarity of her kiss. She'd changed, and it excited me even more as I felt her hand unbutton my jeans.

As I stripped off her clothes, quickly and expertly, she did the same with mine, our breath coming together, hot and wanting as her lips found mine over and over. Her kisses were forceful and deliberate as though she was trying to heal me.

The feel of her soft naked skin erased all the pain I had been carrying around for so long. As her hands found mine, I knew that there was nowhere else I would ever need to be but with her. We were made for one another, and I was reminded of that with every touch. She was the part of me that I had been missing. Our bodies moved together in perfect rhythm as though they were made only for one another, as though we had never been apart. When we had both exploded with our love and passion for one another, we lay panting, exhilarated and exhausted, holding one another as though our lives depended on it.

"I love you, Mags," I sighed, my lips against her shoulder, my heart beating hard against her chest.

"I love you, Sam." It had been so many years since I'd heard those words, and I could feel them move through me, settling in a permanent place in my heart, her soft voice making me realize that I was finally home.

Even though I didn't deserve her she was slowly easing my pain, and as I held her close, I knew that I could never choose to live without her again. She was my life, my love, and my everything.

I had hurt her and nearly destroyed myself in the process, but I knew that I would never again forget that she was the other half of me.

## 32

# EPILOGUE

M ags
Five Years Later

I'VE ALWAYS WANTED TO HAVE AT LEAST THREE CHILDREN,
and Sam and I are nearly there.

At ten, Moira is going to be the best big sister, embracing
the idea of twin siblings far better than I'd ever imagined she
would.

"One for you and one for me," she'd said, smiling, her
beautiful brown eyes dancing with joy.

"What about Dad?" I asked, smiling as I chucked her cute
little chin.

"He has us!" she giggled.

We sat on our back porch, enjoying one of the last of our
peaceful Saturdays before the babies were due to arrive. We'd
finally bought our first home in a quiet city, far from the
gritty neighborhood that Sam had grown up in, and closer to
my parents who seemed even more excited than we were.

A boy and a girl, Alexander and Emma Elizabeth, already so well loved as everyone eagerly anticipated their arrival.

My phone beeped.

"Need anything?" Our new neighbor and fast friend, Madison, was texting me. We had hit it off immediately, my first real female friend, and she couldn't wait to introduce her three-year-old to the babies when they came.

"I'm good," I replied, smiling.

Five years had come and gone so quickly as Sam, Moira, and I tried to settle into a routine of love and forgiveness.

It hadn't been easy in the beginning, Moira more resistant to Sam than either of us had ever expected. Losing Dylan had been devastating for her, and she blamed Sam

"It's all your fault!" she would yell at Sam. "I miss Daddy Dylan! I'd rather have him than you!"

Sam was at a loss about what to do with an angry five-year-old who rebuffed him at every turn.

"I'm sorry, Mo. I'm so sorry," Sam would repeat, finding his own name for her that she allowed. Eventually she softened toward him, but at five she was stubborn, and she punished him for abandoning her before she allowed him in. She knew that he'd had a choice, and she reminded him that it was the wrong one before she let him in.

While I felt sorry for him, I marveled at Moira's wisdom at such a young age to somehow know that she deserved more than what he had given her, and to demand it from him. She wasn't going to forgive him without making sure that he was there to stay.

With much frustration, counseling, and time we had finally found our way, the daily tensions easing slowly as we worked hard to find who we were together.

Moira's anger slowly dissipated as I let go of my own rage, even though it tried to resurface every once in a while. Sam had said "I'm sorry" thousands of times until one day his words finally reached inside and took hold, and we were able to believe him.

We had finally found our normal, and moving into our new home gave us the fresh beginning that we deserved.

The sound of footsteps walking out onto the porch startled me.

"Hi, Maggie." My mom was a welcome sight as she leaned over and kissed me warmly. Moira, thrilled anytime my mom was near, ran to her.

The bond between them had always been special, and with every year, it became even stronger. Moira had changed her, turning her into the mother I'd always yearned for.

"Grandma! Grandpa!"

"Hi, Mom and Dad," I said, attempting to get up, my body refusing to make it easy.

"How's our girl?" my dad said, pulling me up and hugging me tight. "Are you feeling okay?"

He put his hand on my mom's back and I saw it, the love between them palpable, and I smiled.

"I'm good, Daddy," I grunted.

"We put our suitcases in the guest room and are ready to help when the babies come," my mom said, her voice full of excitement. She put her arms around Moira and kissed her head. "We're going to take great care of everyone, aren't we, Moo?"

My mom was now the only one allowed to call Moira by her childhood nickname, and I felt a twinge of jealousy as Moira nodded. "We got you, Mom," she smiled at me.

We sat on the porch and talked, drinking tea as we waited for Sam to come home.

Our family was small, but we had finally found a place of peace and stability, and I was grateful for all we had been through. It was as though we were meant to be here this way, and everything felt right with the world. The tears and the sadness had all been worth it after all.

Sam came home, struggling with bags of groceries. We were battening down the hatches and preparing for the next few weeks to be full of hecticness.

"How's my girl?" Sam asked, his voice warming my heart.

"I'm good," I smiled, touching his face and marveling at how good he looked despite how tired he already was. I hadn't been sleeping well, and Sam woke at every toss and turn of my body. "You?"

"Great!" He exclaimed, kissing my ring finger as he often did. He'd convinced me to put my engagement ring back on, and then in a small ceremony we'd added a wedding band to it. Now my swollen fingers were bare, the rings safely tucked away, but Sam still kissed my ring finger every day as a reminder of where they would sit one day soon.

As I looked at him, a surge of love welled up within me. He had always been with me, buried deep in my heart even before I'd realized who he was. He had taken away my sadness and loneliness, and gave me more happiness than I could ever imagine.

We'd come full circle, healing one another with our love and forgiveness, and a life without him was unimaginable.

A sudden and sharp pain in my stomach nearly knocked me down.

"Oh ... Sam," I breathed clutching my stomach.

In an instant he was by my side.

"Is it time?" he asked, his eyes wide.

"I think so," I said trying to recover from the pain.

Everyone moved quickly, Moira putting the bags in the trunk and my dad helping Sam get me in the car. Within moments we were all on our way to the hospital.

The rest of the day moved slowly as we prepared for the births. Even though we had done everything we could to ready ourselves, the unknown still caused quite a bit of nervousness.

The pain came in waves, the epidural a God-send when they finally administered it. After hours, it became evident to the doctor that the babies weren't going to come the natural way.

"We're going to have to do a C-section," she said briefing us on the why's and what to expect. I nodded fearfully, wanting the best for the babies as Sam squeezed my hands and tried to reassure me that everything was going to be alright.

As they wheeled me into the operating room, Sam by my side, I began to panic. We had always been each other's comfort, neither of us feeling completely safe without the other. I knew that if he was with me that I had nothing to fear, so I closed my eyes, determined to bring my babies into the world with love and positive thoughts.

I suddenly felt my entire body become numb as the medicine they injected me with began to work. The numbness terrified me and I felt trapped in my own body. I began to take deep, long, breaths until I felt myself take control.

After much tugging and pulling, I saw them pull out one baby and then two, both hurried over to separate tables where able hands assessed and cleaned them up. When their cries filled the room, Sam and I cried in relief, neither of us wanting to admit our fear. With multiples, there were risks, but both babies were healthy and well-developed.

For Sam, it was the first time he'd ever experienced birth, and it was both terrifying and magical.

When we held them in our arms for the first time, a love like I'd never imagined came over me. I realized that the life I'd known had never felt complete until Alexander and Emma had arrived. Moira fell in love immediately as she held one then the other.

"They're beautiful," she breathed, kissing them over and over.

As I watched Sam holding Emma, I pushed away a pang of sadness that he'd never held Moira that way. I knew that we were looking ahead, and that dwelling on what never was would prevent our chance at true happiness. The love in his eyes was palpable and real, and as I stared at him, Moira, and the babies together, I had an overwhelming sense of peace.

Everything I'd ever wanted was right there in front me, and it was no longer only Sam who was the other half of me.

My other half also consisted of Moira and the babies, and for the first time in my entire existence, my heart and soul finally felt entirely complete.

The End

<<<<>>>>

# AFTERWORD

Thank you so much for reading The Other Half of Me.

Please help others to find my book by leaving an honest review on Goodreads and on your favorite book-buying platform.

Reviews don't have to be long or detailed. They can be one or two lines that simply state how you felt about the book! It helps readers want to take a chance on a new-to-them author and we appreciate it so very much!

If you'd like to keep up with me, please join my email list and you'll receive a free eCopy of Leaving Eva, the first book in the Eva Series, as well as updates and news about my author journey.

Thank you so much for reading!

X,

Jennifer

# ACKNOWLEDGMENTS

The story of Sam and Maggie began with a completely different idea and evolved into a story of unending love. I've always been drawn to desperate souls and they were no exception. I'm so thankful that I have the opportunity to breathe life into these stories that often begin with just a single idea or thought, and continue to be surprised when people read them.

I'm eternally grateful for my family for giving me the gift of the time to mold these ideas into books. While we juggle our crazy lives, I'm able to steal moments that give me such peace and solitude as I put the words onto paper. I'm beyond thankful that they understand this part of me that I need so much to feel whole.

Throughout this fantastic journey I've met so many people who have become near and dear to my heart.

J.C. Wing, wonderful author, soul sister, and editor, has inspired me and I am ecstatic to have her in my life for more reasons than I can count.

J.M. Walker, author, beautifully talented friend, and cover designer, continues to amaze me with her numerous gifts and kind heart.

My beta readers, Cindi Englehart, Elizabeth Shuey, Edie Knisell, and Heather Simpson, gave me wonderful feedback about this story that helped enrich it and I am grateful for them.

My reader group, Jen's Literary Loves, gives me such joy because they are always so supportive and wonderful. They give me such a sense of direction and purpose that I never could've imagined.

Samantha Soccorso is the best PA and sweet friend, and I'm so grateful for her tireless effort and hard work.

I'm always thankful for my biggest fan, Merikay Walton (my mom) who reads everything I write, even if it's a little out of her wheel- house. I'm so fortunate that I have her support and realize how lucky I am to have a family who understands my need to write the stories that are in my head.

Last but not least, for all of the lost souls who fight hard to find their way home, just know that it's never too late when you have people who love you. Don't ever give up.

## ALSO BY JENNIFER SIVEC

Leaving Eva

Losing Eva

Saving Eva

The Eva Series; the Complete Collection

I Run to You

The Forgotten

The Other Half of Me

The Good One, Part One

The Good One, Part Two

Grey's Harbor Series:

Grey's Landing (Book One)-Lark Griffing

The Grey's Harbor Anthology (Book Two)-JC Wing, Piper Malone,
Carol Cassada, Lark Griffing, Jennifer Sivec

Hope Adrift (Book Three)-Lark Griffing

Harbor Tides (Book Four)-Lark Griffing

Perfect Seas (Book Five)-Jennifer Sivec

(Harbor Song (Book Six)-JC Wing)

A Grey's Harbor Christmas Anthology (Book Seven)-JC Wing, Lark
Griffing, Piper Malone, Jennifer Sivec

# ABOUT THE AUTHOR

Jennifer Sivec writes beautifully broken stories with heart.

She is attracted to and writes stories with characters that are complicated, flawed and completely imperfect. Her books are often a reflection of life, encompassing difficult subjects such as cancer, addiction, abandonment, and abuse. She writes with a raw, complex, yet hopeful approach often weaving tragic stories with honesty and grace, creating unforgettable characters.

Jennifer's passion for reading and sharing stories gives her perspective and peace of mind.

She lives in Ohio with her husband, two boys, and herd of dogs who create balance and levity for her. She loves her crazy life and wonderful readers, and is grateful for all of it, every day.

*For more information about Jennifer:*
www.jennifersivec.com
jennifersivec@yahoo.com

www.ingramcontent.com/pod-product-compliance
Lightning Source LLC
Chambersburg PA
CBHW072140170626
46813CB00004BA/1630